A NIGHT OF SCREAMS

LATINO HORROR STORIES

LATINO HORROR STORIES

EDITED BY
RICHARD Z. SANTOS

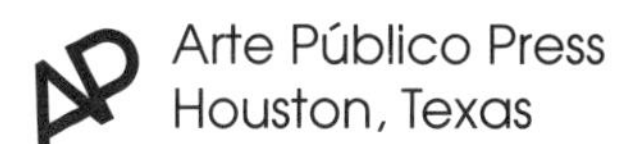

Recovering the past, creating the future

Arte Público Press
University of Houston
4902 Gulf Fwy, Bldg 19, Rm 100
Houston, Texas 77204-2004

Cover design by Mora Des¡gn
Cover art by Adobe Stock

Names: Santos, Richard Z., editor.
Title: A night of screams : Latino horror stories / edited by Richard Z. Santos. Description: Houston, Texas : Arte Público Press, [2023] | Summary: "The movement of the old woman's hands is quick and youthful as she works the dough for tamales on Mars' dusty, dry surface where their cohete broke apart and crash landed. She, her husband and their only son survive, and the old man curses the coyotes who took his money for a rocket not built to accommodate his family of eleven. A storm is coming, and he rails at his wife that she's wasting her time. "We'll be dead by the time you finish your goddamn tamales." This riveting collection of horror stories-and four poems-contains a wide range of styles, themes and authors. Creepy creatures roam the pages, including La Llorona and the Chupacabras in fresh takes on Latin American lore, as well as ghosts, zombies and shadow selves. Migrants continue to pass through Rancho Altamira where Esteban's family has lived for generations, but now there are two types: the living and the dead. A young man returns repeatedly to the scary portal down which his buddy disappeared. A woman is relieved to receive multiple calls from her cousin following Hurricane María in Puerto Rico, but she is stunned to later learn her prima died the first night of the storm! There's plenty of blood and gore in some stories, while others are mysterious and suspenseful. In his introduction, editor Richard Z. Santos writes it is no surprise these stories are brilliant and terrifying, given cartel violence, a history of CIA-backed dictatorships in Latin America, increasingly scary rhetoric from American politicians, decades of institutionalized racism and the demonization of Latinos in the media. "After all," he says, "we are the faceless horde, invading zombies hellbent on upturning the world and replacing it with something foreign, accented and impossibly different""-- Provided by publisher.
Identifiers: LCCN 2022060538 (print) | LCCN 2022060539 (ebook) | ISBN 9781558859616 (paperback ; alk. paper) | ISBN 9781518507519 (epub) | ISBN 9781518507526 (kindle edition) | ISBN 9781518507533 (pdf)
Subjects: LCSH: Horror tales, American. | Latin Americans--Fiction. | Folklore--Latin America--Fiction. | American fiction--Hispanic American authors. | LCGFT: Horror fiction. | Short stories. | Poetry.
Classification: LCC PS648.H6 N494 2023 (print) | LCC PS648.H6 (ebook) | DDC 813/.087308868073--dc23/eng/20230307
LC record available at https://lccn.loc.gov/2022060538
LC ebook record available at https://lccn.loc.gov/2022060539

∞ The paper used in this publication meets the requirements of the American National Standard for Information Sciences—Permanence of Paper for Printed Library Materials, ANSI Z39.48-1984.

22 23 24 4 3 2 1

Contents

Dedicated to those reading under a blanket with a flashlight. That noise you heard is probably nothing. Hopefully.

Introduction by Richard Z. Santos

Something is happening to horror writing. Over the past few years, a new breed of writers has edged out the established names and tired horror tropes and brought horror into the twenty-first century on a wave of gore, quiet scares and, sometimes, literary respect. Writers of color have played a huge role in the continued evolution of the horror genre.

People have been writing scary stories forever, but the success of Stephen King, Peter Straub, Lisa Tuttle, Clive Barker and others in the 1980s and 1990s announced horror as a viable and profitable genre. This era fully brought scary stories out of pulp magazines and cheap paperbacks into the mainstream. Since then, authors have continued to challenge genre labels and strike out into new territory. Today, you can walk into just about any bookstore and find a range of books pushing the boundaries of what we call horror.

If you want literary horror with only traces of the supernatural, or scary stories about ghosts or demonic possession or slasher books, it's all there and a lot of it is really good. Produced by major publishers, micro presses, self-published books, horror is everywhere and it's not only growing; it is evolving.

Even the works of those four I mentioned at the top—King, Straub, Tuttle and Barker—became less scary, but no less unsettling, as they and their writing matured. Many horror classics from a few decades ago (such as *The October Country* by Ray

Bradbury or *We Have Always Lived in the Castle* by Shirley Jackson) have slipped out of the horror category and are now considered literary fiction or psychological thrillers.

That's why I consider this book more than a collection of horror stories. Today, we have writers who work in horror while combining elements of fantasy, science fiction, magical realism and literary fiction, making their books more weird or unsettling than scary. Of course, there are other writers who just want to make you look over your shoulder, wonder what that noise in the hallway is and regret opening their book when the house is dark, quiet and (hopefully) empty.

This collection includes all of the above. There are horror stories meant to send a shiver down your spine. But there are also quieter stories that want to unsettle you more than scare you. These weird tales present a world that is $9/10^{th}$ the same as ours . . . but that $1/10^{th}$ difference is more than enough.

Latinos have specifically carved out a space for themselves in this new morphing, hybrid market. And honestly, why wouldn't we be good at writing scary stories that challenge traditional narrative structures?

We read Stephen King back when he was trashy. At the same time, we were reading Gabriel García Márquez's tales about flying people, Toni Morrison's ghost stories and Kurt Vonnegut's science fiction—all of which felt more real and true than most of what gets passed off for realism now or then. We were told bedtime stories about kids being drowned in the river near our house—or for you was it a pond, or a drainage ditch, or an arroyo? As we grew up, family movie nights might have evolved from *Godzilla vs Megalon* to the horror films of Santo, to *Ghostbusters*, to *Halloween*, *Santa Sangre*, *Cronos* and *The Orphanage*. Most of us watched *The X Files*, *Buffy* and all their imitators, and lots of us listened to violent music that glamorized criminals, torture and death—I'll let you decide if I'm referring to gangsta rap or *narcocorridos*.

Take this cultural stew and throw in cartel violence in Mexico, a history of CIA-backed dictatorships in Central and South America, increasingly scary rhetoric from American politicians, decades of institutionalized racism, the demonization of our families on the most popular networks on television, and how could the result be anything other than brilliant, terrifying stories? After all, we are the faceless horde, invading zombies hell bent on upturning the world and replacing it with something foreign, accented and impossibly different.

Many fans and writers of horror feel safer inside these works because they are less scary than what's actually out there. Give me the ghost of a child trapped in a well over a lunatic with a machine gun walking into a school any day of the week.

The original idea for this collection was to showcase new works that explored the notion of hybridity. The experience of Latinx people in the United States is one of hybrid languages, religions, cultures and customs. Even at an institutional level we're straddling worlds.

I taught in high school for many years, and time and again I had to help kids fill out PSAT registration forms or some other bureaucratic nonsense. So many students would get stuck on the demographic questions. I had to explain to them that there's no Latino "race" and they were expected to select white. The confused, offended look in their eyes wouldn't have been much different if I had told them they were secretly a werewolf or a wizard. That is, after all, one of the classic horror situations. You thought you were one thing your whole life . . . and then you learn the truth.

As a group, we can't even fully decide if we are a group, and, if we are, what to call ourselves. Some of you reading these pages bristled at my use of "Latinx"—so new, so not-Spanish—

two paragraphs ago. Others sighed when I invoked the sexist dinosaur that is "Latino." Well, this book also contains Latines, Chicanas, Tejanos, Nuyoricans, Hispanics (Gasp!), BIPOCs, writers of color, combinations of the above and more. As a group, we struggle to label ourselves because so much life, history and color can't fit into five or six letters. How can a writer of Afro-Cuban descent living in New York City agree to the same label as a resident of the Rio Grande Valley whose family has lived there since before the United States and Mexico existed?

We have no label, and I don't think this particular story will ever end. There's not going to be a magical combination of letters we all agree on. No spell will bind us into one unit because the words can't contain us. Even how we use those words differs from person to person. You'll notice in this anthology that about half the pieces use italicized Spanish and about half do not. We left this choice up to the author.

Even scarier, is there actually an "us"? Can *Latinidad* really include socialists from the Bronx, Trump voters from Laredo, immigrants, immigrant haters, devout Catholics, atheists and every other polar opposite plus all the gradations in between?

Chicana scholar Gloria Anzaldúa famously described the US-Mexico border as "*una herida abierta* where the Third World grates against the first and bleeds. And before a scab forms it hemorrhages again, the lifeblood of two worlds merging to form a third country—a border culture" (*The Borderlands/La Frontera.*)

Anzaldúa was writing from a very specific perspective as a queer Mexican-American woman in Texas, but the notion of a new border culture extends beyond the literal US-Mexico border all the way across this country and into all the emotional and psychological borderlands. Those open wounds are present everywhere the labels don't fit, the language doesn't sound right and we become aware of our differences.

We are here, unnameable, unsettled, at odds with ourselves and with everyone else.

Scary.

Editor's Note

There's a little bit of everything in here: zombies, ghosts, a *chupacabra* (or two), shadow selves, mysterious portals, cable news hosts, ancient spirits, old magic and new.

While putting this collection together, I posted an open call for submissions. This book includes several pieces that came in from the "slush pile," which is such a scary, slimy name for a place full of so many wonders. I also personally reached out to writers and asked each to submit a piece. This included writers established in the horror genre and those entering these dark waters for the first time.

My goal was to put together a collection that included everything from blood and guts to campfire ghost stories, to subtle works that reveled in language and explored the great mysteries of life and death.

Several stories provide new takes on classic Mexican and Mexican-American folk tales, such as "Dark Lord of the Rainbow", "The Boy Called Chupa" by V. Castro and "A Curious Encounter" by mónica teresa ortíz. These tales are so familiar and almost comforting, yet so new and fresh. "La Llorona Happenings" by Flor Salcedo and "Chola Salvation" by Estella Gonzalez present dazzling new takes on some of the most important women in Latino culture.

Cloud Cardona and Ruben Quesada provided poems that touch on life, death and what comes after. These are two of my favorite writers, and I think their work fits right alongside the bloodier, more direct pieces.

Speaking of blood, there's plenty to be found in Rubén Degollado's zombie story "Migrants," which is Rubén's first horror story. Also new to the genre is Oscar Mancinas, whose story "Cruz and Me" is about the mystery of friendship (and a scary portal to somewhere else). The two best friends in Adrian Ernesto Cepeda's "A Night of Screams in Austin, TX" find themselves someplace they knew they shouldn't have gone. Leticia Urieta's "Detached" is a piece of bloody body horror, and I swear you'll be able to *hear* wet footsteps while reading this one.

Pedro Iniguez's "Purveyors and Puppets" explores the dark side to one of this nation's most frightening inventions: cable news. Haunted artists play a key part in Richie Narvaez's Faustian tale "A Thing with Feathers," and the singer in Lilliam Rivera's "Between Going and Staying" discovers that success can only keep her away from her family for so long.

As in many pieces of Latino literature, the role of family runs throughout nearly all these pieces. "Indian Blood" by Marcos Damián León is not only about the horrors of being broke but also the pressure of our heritage. Ann Dávila Cardinal's "What the Hurricane Took" uses only dialogue to bring the horror of Hurricane María's effect on Puerto Rico to life. Cardinal's story, like others here, focuses on the truly scary part of tragedy—what happens next.

The sci-fi tragedy "Tamales" by José Alaniz is one of the most unsettling pieces in this book, and I don't know how else to describe it other than saying: Mars, tamales, a *cohete* and a storm. The main character in Sydney Macias's "It Said 'Bellevue' " has found a family of sorts among the mistakes, miracles and demons kept hidden underneath that famous hospital. There are several found families in Toni Margarita Plummer's "Night Shifts," which features a very old character dealing with modern versions of timeless problems.

Ivelisse Rodriguez closes the collection with a story that brings many strands of Latino culture, history and spirituality together and miraculously leaves the door open for a way to undo so many horrors.

Thank you to everyone who submitted, to those who suggested writers for me to reach out to and to those who encouraged this project.

I think the people I have given the biggest nightmares to are Dr. Nicolás Kanellos, Marina Tristán, Gabi Baeza Ventura and the rest of the Arte Público crew who had to deal with my delays, uncertainties and bad organizational skills. Thank you for your patience and seeing this through.

And, of course, thank you for being the kind of person who reads every intro, author's note, bio and more. We need more people like you out there.

Dark Lord of the Rainbow

Monique Quintana

When you're nine, your grandmother tells you the story about the Rainbow Ballroom to scare you. She tells you the story while making you a Shirley Temple right before bedtime. She uses a tiny glass jam jar instead of a cup. The way the story goes, she says, there was a teenage girl who met a beautiful man in the ballroom, and he asked her to go on a moonlit drive. Your grandmother tells you this is where she goes wrong. She should have stayed there with her friends. She's lucky she got to go out in the first place. Your grandmother drops a cherry in your soda, and you watch the fizz come up the jar like an amoeba. That should have been enough fun for her, your grandmother tells you.

The girl looks down and sees the man has hooves where his feet should be. No one ever sees the girl again. You ask your grandmother how she or anyone, for that matter, could know the man had hooved feet if the girl had disappeared? Your grandmother doesn't answer your question. She shakes her way out of the kitchen and into her garden.

Your grandmother will take you to visit your aunt's house in Parkside. While your grandmother's talking to her sister in the kitchen, your cousin invites you to her bedroom, and under her canopy, puffy, like clouds, you sit on her bed and tell her about the beautiful man with hooved feet. Your cousin is seven years older and has Spaniard skin and hair blacker than your own. Yes, she tells you. She sticks her finger in the dimple on her face. There was such a man with hooves where his feet should be. Everyone knows the story because the girl danced all night with him. She came home with the rain in her hair and blisters on her feet, and tequila in her mouth, and then your cousin taps your throat with her fingertips, and they burn there like three sticks of copal.

The girl has curly hair like you and is as dark as you. She irons her hair before she goes out, the way you do now. There is a disco ball with green and yellow lights. The woman wears a red polyester dress that feels like silk in your hands. You wrap the dress around her breasts and ribs and her empty womb. You tie the dress in ribbons at her thighs. The beautiful man finds her and asks her to dance. He smells like pricy cologne and leather, and his hair is slicked black over his ear lobes, and the sun has scorched his skin the way you like it. He speaks to her in Spanish. You don't know how to speak Spanish, so the girl hears his words in reverse, and she reads his intentions on his fingertips as they run up her back. The girl leaves with the man in his Chevy Malibu. The air is warm and slow bleeding with rain. Fingers fall on the skin. The buildings go by in pitch and blue and trees and dust. She looks down at the gas pedal. She looks down to where his feet should be. She knows—the moon tips over his hooves and sighs.

Migrants

Rubén Degollado

As the day was ending, Esteban decided to check the trap on the easternmost end of Rancho Altamira, where his family had lived for generations. His grandfather Esequiel Barajas had built the ranch decades before the world changed, and Esteban was glad he had gone to San Pedro's gates in heaven before all this. The trap was empty with no feral hog or javelina, and the trail of corn leading to the cage was uneaten. Where the feral hogs had been a nuisance across the border land, and ranchers and farmers had paid hunters to bag them, they were now scarce, hunted out by the living or devoured by roving droves of the dead. If the other trap to the south was also empty, he'd have to eat what was left of the javelina stew he'd made, which would only be good for another day or so. Esteban checked the cage for its functioning. It had a large opening big enough for an adult hog, where they were enticed to enter for the corn and figs he'd laid in the trough. On the ground, near the feeder, there was a steel plate attached to a taut wire. When the animal stepped on this, it would pull a pin wedged between the bottom of the door and the top of the cage. He stuck the muzzle of his cuerno through the bars and tapped the plate. The door came screeching down to the ground. Gracias a Dios, it was still working and at least there was that. He checked the trough. The figs and corn were still there, untouched, other than scores of flies which were ever present. He reset the trap and walked away.

Esteban walked out of the brush and back onto the sendero. There were no deer or javelina tracks or the skip dragging parallel foot tracks of los muertos. He stopped to listen, and at first all he could hear was the chicharras and a little breeze stirring in the mesquite trees. It was when he held his breath that he heard groaning in the wind, and he knew the trap to the south of the house needed attending to.

He came to the last deer blind before the road leading up to the house, and he still hadn't found any tracks, except for the zigzag lines of a rattler and the tiny stars of roadrunners. This blind was hardly more than a plywood box painted green. It was at the intersection of two paths, which gave anyone inside two angles to shoot from. When his family had leased out the land, and the deer were plentiful and hunting was a sport and not a necessity, it had been the second-best blind. The favorite had been the tower, a twenty-foot-high steel blind that had vantage across the entire ranch. He opened the blind door and searched for scorpions and black widows on the dirty carpet floor. There were none, so he grabbed the milk jug filled with water he had left for the migrants passing through. He opened it, sniffed at it and drank anyway, regardless of how stale it smelled. With the family's well and the windmill to run it, clean water was still plentiful, at least on his ranch. There were milk jugs like this across their acreage laid out for the caravans of living people passing through, on their way to a better life and security beyond the wall. Years ago, his grandfather had dug a hundred feet down past the water table, and the aquifer beneath their land was plentiful. Esteban had enough to be generous. He traded the water for gun powder, lead from wheel weights for casting bullets and shell casings; he was able to reload in the popular calibers of 9mm, 5.56 and 7.62x39, and trade the Golfos for canned food and alcohol. This exchange also provided Esteban the protection of Chuy and his men from other cartels who might try to come in and steal whatever Esteban had. It was an uneasy alliance, sure, but Chuy had been a friend to the Barajas family, and the other soldiers respected the generational arrangement. They had even given him the cuerno, a Romanian-made AKM he kept running with his own reloads, lubricated with liquefied pig fat, and he only used it on deer and the dead.

The Golfos had done their business on his land when mostly what used to go north was product and what came south was cash. But now it was people, and even that had slowed as they had either given up because of the border wall or had settled in where they were, resigned that they would just have to make a go of it. Fight the living for food and water and the dead for the safety of their own bodies, such as they were.

The javelina he used to attract muertos was safe in the cage next to the corral trap, even as a dead one crouched on the ground and snapped at it, breaking its teeth on the hog panel, ripping the flesh of its face away. It was a migrant or coyote who had made it this far but would make it no further. Esteban whistled at it, and its dead eyes flicked in his direction. It was penned in the corral a living person could have easily scaled, but once life had left them, they lost the sense or coordination to do the simplest things. He could have ended it without noise, but needed to test his recent batch of reloads, and so he leveled the cuerno and lowered the heavy safety. The shot dropped it easily. Esteban was thankful he had not missed. One shot from the cuerno was good, but a second shot would give a location to other muertos where they would come seeking dinner.

And it was then that living people came out of brush and tried to run away from him. It was a risk to make more noise, but he yelled at them to stop.

There were about fifteen of them—men, women and teens—all migrants fixing masks to their faces, not a coyote in sight and no one stepping forward as the leader. Esteban kept the rifle on them and yelled in Spanish for them to all stop. They had set up a camp there, waiting for night to make the crossing to avoid the patrols guarding the river. From the fresh scrape marks on the trap door's padlock, it was obvious they had also tried to get to the bait javelina, in competition with the muerto in the corral.

They complied and were still and seemed relieved he hadn't killed them.

They ignored the question and said, "We are looking for food and water, and were wondering if you had anything before heading on."

"Let me ask again. Where is your coyote? Who is leading you across?"

Despite the cuerno pointing their way, they stepped forward and told him they were hungry. "Por favor," they said.

Esteban raised the rifle higher. He said, "Where. Is. Your. Coyote?"

A man in the front pointed to the corral. "He is there. That was him. We got separated from him earlier, and there he is now."

If it was him, it was one of Chuy's men whom Esteban didn't recognize. Without the coyote on Chuy's payroll, these migrants would never make it to the other side.

Esteban flipped the safety up on the cuerno and slipped his head through the sling. He was not dropping his guard, and he reached down and rested his hand on the Browning at his waistband, both as a warning and as a precaution. If they rushed him at this distance, the pistol would be a better weapon, one they would have a harder time grabbing away from him. And if he ran out of bullets, the machete would work as well.

"So, you are the leader now."

The man shrugged.

"Have your people sit down here on the ground and tell them not to get up. Behind me are some jugs of water in a blind. You get that for your people and then you stay here with them. And if any of you follow me to the house, I will drop you where you stand."

Esteban backed up a few feet and watched as each of them slipped off their backpacks and eased their bodies to the ground.

When he came back with tacos filled with the javelina guisado that was only slightly turned, he counted each head, and they were all still there. He bid the leader to come forward and take the food.

The man distributed a foil wrapped taco—mainly tortillas smeared with guisado gravy—to each of the migrants and they pulled off their masks, some with gray N95s, others with bandanas and makeshift shemaghs. They ate them in silence, and he saw a few of them hiccup as they drank water from the jugs he'd provided.

As they sat on the ground eating their tacos, Esteban said, "Once it gets dark, it will be time to go. You head back down that road and cut across to the sendero that runs parallel up to our fence line. Whatever you do, stay off the main road. There might be men on patrol, and if you get seen, they won't be offering you tacos. You're on your own now that the coyote is dead."

"Thank you, compa. I'll get my people moving."

"Is it that bad?" Esteban said and pointed his chin in the direction from which they had come.

"Compa, you have no idea how bad it is."

"It is not much better over there, but I get it, it's still better. They still have power."

"It is either risk starving or getting eaten, compa. At least over there on the other side we can find work. At least over there they had better controls in place to keep the dead from overtaking them."

Esteban said, "If God wills it."

The leader said, "Yes, if God wills it."

In the pause when both men wondered what to say next, Esteban heard the dead coming through the brecha and into the clearing. Their sound was unmistakable, the sad groaning they made only when approaching the living, the tattered clothes catching on huisache thorns, the shuffle of their feet that never left the ground.

Esteban yelled, "Move!" But it was too late. They were already on top of them, their teeth searching for exposed flesh and finding it. The migrants who were seated and unable to get up in time were the first to be consumed. They lost chunks of skin, the thin bones in their forearms exposed as they tried to defend themselves. There were dozens of them, much more in one place than Esteban had seen in months. Esteban unslung the cuerno and dropped two of them in quick succession. Most of the muertos fixed their decaying eyes his way and moved toward him. The other dead ones, excited by the chase, followed the migrants as they ran toward the wall, hoping against hope to be able to make the crossing at dusk, pass through the opening where the money to build the wall had run out. Esteban sprayed the air to get the herd's attention, but the ones who had the migrants in their sights were undeterred as they shambled after them. Esteban then realized the only hope for him was to run to the tower.

The tower was a twenty-foot-high deer blind positioned in the center of the ranch, on a moderate hill. Esteban kept the blind stocked with water and full magazines for the cuerno on the platform in an ammo can he'd hauled up there. It was the place for a last stand. If Esteban couldn't clear the muertos at the base, he would be able to hold out until Chuy's men came to his aid when they heard the reports of his shots. Esteban looked below and there were more muertos than he had thought, enough to encircle the base of the blind, close to thirty or so of them. As he loaded a fresh magazine and prepared himself to clear them, he looked to the wall and saw what was left of the caravan approaching it. The light was failing, but there was enough for him to see them. They were nowhere near the opening in the wall and couldn't see it from their vantage point as the wall curved around beyond them to the west. Desperate, with the dead behind them, getting closer and about to trap them against the wall, he watched them do their best to scale the rusty slats to make the crossing to the safety that lay beyond. Like all the caravans of desperate people who had come before, both before and after the fall, the migrants believed this risk was better than what was behind them. Esteban wanted to call to them, tell them which way to go, convince them that what they were doing was impossible, that they would fall to their deaths. But the wind would block his voice as it had blocked the sounds of the herd, just like the wall blocked their passage now. As he saw the migrants failing the climb, others indecisive on which way to run, the muertos overcame them. The battalion of the dead—now joined by the freshly reanimated migrants—pulled them down and devoured them where they fell. Esteban thought about how brave they were to have made it this far, to fight so valiantly to the very end, but how cruel it was to have gotten so close to the refuge of Mexico, only to be blocked by the wall that had been built to keep them safe from it.

La Llorona Happenings

Flor Salcedo

The rickety, metal screen door hadn't even snapped my backside yet, but Mom's glare had already trapped me as I set foot into our apartment. She clicked the off switch to our second-hand vacuum cleaner and went into a low-growl sermon. "*¡Mírate!*" she snapped with a nun's restrained authority. "You're only eight, *muchachita*, but think you can be out late. La Llorona might come get you and drag you to the river."

I was frozen at the narrow landing at the bottom of the stairwell which led up to our second floor, same as every other unit in the Salazar Apartments, or how we called them—the projects. I was like an alien specimen, the bright lights highlighting my tanned skin against the white wall. Mom had said many times before that I was all hair, scrapes and bony knees.

Mom tap-tapped a few steps closer to me in her huarache sandals. I stared at the torn corner of the prickly-pear-red rug with the big yellow flowers, the rug mom vacuumed daily because she couldn't keep the dirt away. I had told her before to just close the windows, but she wanted air coming into our cramped apartment, even if it was dusty, desert air. Mom got a faraway look as she continued the story of the crying lady. "The woman *está llorando* y *llorando* for all eternity." Her tongue snagged over the English words as she stressed "eternity".

Gosh, that's a lot of crying.

I ignored the first, second, maybe even third and fourth time Mom had yelled for me. Night brought out the scents of mesquite trees and cool dirt. I roamed the darkness like a bewitched owl. I wanted to keep playing outside close to the Rio Grande River that swelled with yesterday's rain, the humidity that was still dry somehow because we lived in the desert. The skinny river looked more like a stream near my house and didn't stay filled for long thanks to the griddle-hot sun. The neighborhood kids and I, we ran around like a wild pack of wolves—muddy shoes, torn shirts, skirts, elbows, legs, browns and tans, boys, girls, five-year-olds to teens. "Those *chavalos* and *chavalas* are just *chusma*," Mom would always grumble. I would shrug away her dislike of my clan. Those kids shared my nighttime thrill, and in our nightly sprees, I had sometimes smirked and whispered to my *chusma*, "La Llorona's coming to get you." Dark brown faces of kids that had been out in the sun all summer peered in the shadows. White teeth gleamed, then there were snickers and rolling eyes, but they turned to check behind themselves anyway.

Mom scrunched her lips with calm impatience at me zoning out of her lesson. She sat in front of the oscillating floor fan pointed to her favorite corner couch. Her calf-length cotton night robe fell loose on her curves, curlers tightly wound in her hair, sharp crow eyes beamed in on me. She rubbed off the dust that had settled on her nose and, with the help of sweeping hand movements, told the tale like an expert frightener. La Llorona's spirit lamented drowning her children and traveled non-stop up and down the river in her long, flowy, gown. Mom stumbled over the conflicting versions people had as to why she drowned them. She sided with the one where the woman lost her mind after her husband left her for another and then committed familicide, taking her own life after drowning her two children.

Mom said I was suitable. Suitable enough for La Llorona to snatch up because I was still a small child. That she took children to pretend they were her own and then drowned them. Made no sense but that was the story.

Another night came, another talk of La Llorona.

And another.

And another.

Little did I know, I'd come to hear the story until I could recite it like the A-B-Cs. Decades later, the projects of the El Paso, Texas desert still lived inside me. *El río* which had been a hop and skip from my house, continued to flow in my dreams. For many years, the river had been a source of stories, a landmark, a divider between the US and Mexico and a source of vitality for people. I remembered well that, for my mom, it became an aid to make her point.

I didn't believe at first, but even my two sisters were afraid of La Llorona at the time, and they were in middle school. It was undeniable when I started to hear her cries myself, drifting from outside as clear as the neighborhood's brawling cats. Soon, women wearing gowns frightened me, particularly if the hemlines looked very dragged and frayed.

The night no longer held the same freedoms. When I bolted to the edge of the neighborhood to throw away the trash bags, they bumped against my legs, spilling some of the mushy food, empty bottles and Kotex napkins. The community dumpster—a giant hunk of metal—smelled so vile, one practically had to do a run-by and toss the bags. For me, the incentive was stronger—rush my skinny behind back home and away from La Llorona if she happened to be prowling nearby.

When La Llorona's wails started up, the peach fuzz on my arms stood on end. Mom's eyes flitted to the window. She'd run around the house, hair still in rollers, shutting the drapes with frantic tugs. My usually chattering sisters would shut up as if on command, their eyes would widen and they'd remain in their spots on the living room couches with tight faces and still bodies. I'd jet to my parent's closet, bury myself behind Mom's dresses and Dad's suits, the familiar cloths wrapping me like a cup of Abuelita's hot chocolate.

I'd tiptoe down the stairs and peer into the living room where my sisters remained as frozen as I had left them, watching their television shows like zombies. Even at that young age, I knew my gossipy sisters well. This was no act. They couldn't possibly keep up a charade this long without cracking a smile.

It went on for months—the sudden cries from outside and my mother hopping into action like a startled lizard.

When I finally couldn't take the routine of running away from the wails and waiting in hidden darkness for them to stop, I did the unthinkable. One afternoon, when La Llorona started up outside with faint sobs, I carefully checked that Mom was still showering and made sure my sisters were as engrossed with the *novela* they were watching as they appeared to be. I scrambled to the kitchen. It was now or never.

I pulled myself up to the sink slowly and methodically, sliding my limbs across the kitchen counter. The metal sink gave a faint creak. I hung to the edge, suspended, waiting to see if anyone heard, and then pulled up against the window, my face brushing the ratty yellow curtains. The kitchen window had a good view of the entire piece of concrete slab that made up our back porch, and even my neighbor's slab. I grasped a curtain edge with trembling hands and pulled.

Just a crack. Just a peek at the monster that was outside.

My heart threatened to rip out of my chest. *¡Híjole!* She really was there. La Llorona, on my neighbor's porch. I was only feet from the abomination.

She was hairy, arachnid-like. She moved in a crouched position, bobbing, crawling, swinging one leg and then the other as she crossed the neighbor's patio, thighs and shoulders glistening in the sunlight. Her contorted mouth was open, caught in an impending wail. The stories had not done justice to her horror.

But, there was a lot of skin. Too much skin. She wasn't wearing any clothes.

Maybe her dress washed away in the river? Even though she's a spirit? Well, dresses do get heavy when wet.

I was stuck in a catch fire of speculation, trying to conceive how a spirit loses her dress, when the scream finally escaped her. The voice was familiar. And then the face.

Eloísa. It was my neighbor's teenage daughter.

Eloísa was doing a half crawl on the concrete floor. Her long, black hair draped like a wet spider web over her shoulders and chest. As she cried in terror, her mouth formed an old lady's grimace. My muscles twitched and my brain melted.

Eloísa threw her arms up in front of herself to cover her face. La Llorona must be trying to drag her away, I was convinced. But it made no sense; Eloísa wasn't a young kid anymore.

A spray of water hit Eloísa and she screeched at the top of her lungs, blurting gibberish. With only the glass window to muffle the sound, it soon became decipherable.

"No, Daddy," she pleaded. "Stop it, Daddy."

Mr. Manchego, my neighbor and her dad, stood like a fireman on a mission, holding a garden hose and spraying her. Hard. She flopped about on the porch, but he was relentless.

There was no Llorona. No spirit. No cursed legend. Just people.

I knew then my sisters really were afraid, just not of the so-called spirit woman.

"Pleeeease," Eloísa screamed. She finally balled up in a corner until it stopped.

I remained transfixed, squatting on top of the sink, my legs tingling like a nest of disturbed fire ants. My fingers must have still been pinching the curtains, but were too numb to feel it. A heavy feeling that I was being watched dug into my neck and I let go of the curtains. I turned toward the figure at the corner of my eye, my body washing over in a cold sweat. My mother stood at the kitchen entrance, watching me, so still and stoic she might've been a statue.

A breath pushed out of my lungs and I waited for a punishment. There was something in Mom's eyes I couldn't understand. She cast her sight to the floor and walked away.

For years, the cries from my neighbor's back porch continued. Sometimes it was Eloísa, sometimes it was Carmen, her older sister—their father dragging them outside naked to hose them down while the neighborhood listened—Eloísa screaming like a toddler, Carmen muttering *pinchi pinchi* curses. There were blessed gaps of months when it didn't happen. But it always returned.

Everyone's silence about the matter burned a hole inside of me. It was clear by everyone's zipped lips we were supposed to pretend it wasn't happening. But every time it did, I was powerless, an endless abyss of anxious worry. It never occurred to me that things could be different. It never occurred to me that I could speak up.

Any time I crossed paths with Carmen and Eloísa, when they were on their way to school or church, I'd tilt my head, spin around, move closer. Anything to make eye contact.

Eloísa always seemed to have a sniffle just waiting to escape her. Her eyes searched the ground in a continuous loop. How badly I wanted to see her black irises. I remembered from before how they had once glimmered like a placid lake. But I couldn't reach them anymore. Still, her face radiated beauty. An Aztec goddess.

Carmen, older by a year or two, had light, golden-brown skin and hazel eyes. She always looked straight ahead. Always. Her eyes were bubbling volcanoes, waiting to spit fire.

In the evenings, I'd go on missions. Simply crossing the wide street behind the apartment complex and going under the border freeway underpass had me halfway there. Then it was just a hop over rusty train tracks and onto a rock embankment, sliding down a few feet of sloped riverbank and *bam,* the trickle of Rio Grande slithered lazily at my feet. I no longer went just to scoop up the tadpoles to take them home and watch them grow legs before releasing them into the yard. I went to peer around the curves, past the thorny bushes that filled the riverbank, hoping I could spot La Llorona. The real one. Perhaps La Llorona just needed someone to talk to.

I saw a draped woman once. She stood blurry in the distance on the dry riverbed, heavily wrapped in cloths, looking my way. I kept still until she seemingly floated away. I pushed down the mix of fear and disappointment.

When I started middle school, and the two neighbor girls went to high school, the screaming continued, but it had moved inside the house. The arguing and fighting was a family affair. Sometimes it was the dad or the mom or Carmen, but hardly ever Eloísa. Over time Carmen would roar above her parent's voices.

One day the fighting stopped altogether. Soon after, my family moved away from the cookie-cutter, low-income units by the river.

"Will the Llorona disappear from my life?" I asked the *chavalos* and *chavalas* on my final day as we walked around the neighborhood together one last time, hands in pockets and kicking rocks.

One of them murmured. "Ey, La Llorona will follow you always. Sorry, yo."

I gulped but accepted this as truth and then hugged them goodbye.

The river was at a surprising mid-level that day when we drove away next to it. The gray waters still and dank.

We left the neighborhood, left the stories behind.

I find myself driving to the projects, searching out the bittersweet memories they hold. Candy knives on my tongue.

As I stand on the dirt in front of the side-by-side apartments that once held my family and the Manchego's, I wish with all my might that Carmen finally slapped the living daylights out of her parents and ran away, taking her sister with her.

Among the community along the river is where folklore seeped into our lives. Sometimes it came in a good way like enchanted desert nights. Sometimes it came like dirty water.

Over the years the area continues changing, many of the apartments taken down, buried under concrete freeway. But the river remains, witness to the crimes of time.

I wonder if Carmen and Eloísa have returned to the place of their violent upbringing. I want to know if Carmen's eyes still burn or if they've extinguished. Has Eloísa ever been able to raise her gaze to the world? Will I ever be able to swallow the silence that we kept while La Llorona happenings took place?

When the Rio Grande swells up and the wind howls, others shush each other and prick an ear, swearing they hear the mourning spirit crying outside, roaming, wallowing in her despair and searching for children to snatch up.

As for me, I hear Carmen and Eloísa.

What I Know

Cloud Cardona

All I know about Tío Raul and my bisabuela Jesusita
is from the warped mirrors of loved ones.

Sometimes I wish I could rip the veil
between this world and the next

ask my tío to tell me about the time he met
? and the Mysterians. Look at my bisabuela

while she tells me about her childhood in Hondo.
I want to know them myself. All I know

is from stray photos tucked away
in my family's dresser. My uncle's pictures

of the backs of heads at a Cher drag show in
the middle of a mall. Jesusita with her white

curls against the blue couch sprawling
with fields of gray floral print.

I know they would love me
but would they like me?

Today, all I know is emails and waiting.
I remind my students to write

in complete sentences while quackgrass
sprouts outside between slabs

of southside cement.
All I know I do miss

everything I don't know. I take in
the brief silence in my classroom

and wait to hear the unfamiliar
whispers of antepasados—

Eternal Life

Cloud Cardona

In Catholic school, I learned
about eternity. I learned that
eternity in heaven is a gift. A privilege
afforded to the well-behaved.
I pictured day after day in the clouds,
running out of things to do.
How was this supposed to be
a gift? I used to stay up staring
at shut blinds, spiraling
about living in endless light.
I asked adults and friends.
I tried Google. It was all the same.
Some ideas are too big
for our brains to wrap around.
So I kept my fears wrapped
up inside me. I pictured time
slinking off each step into the dark
ahead of me. My adolescent bedtime ritual
meant creating images of the grief, the pain,the
waxy bodies of loved ones. I counted all the

ghosts I was bound to meet, mourning my
living loved ones while stray dogs wandered
through my neighborhood. How I envied them.
I envied their
circling of broken sidewalks. I envied
their sleeping on sun-stained grass.
I envied their obscurity
of what I wished
was obscured in me.

The Boy Called Chupa

V. Castro

A fence is not a pillow and he was told there were no pillows left for him. His head continued to bob up and down as he ventured in and out of nightmare-filled sleep leaning against metal that felt cold against his face. His tummy was rumbly and hungry. All he wanted was Mama. His name was Julio, but in his family they called him Chupa. Soon it would be time for his medicine, but it was the medicine only his uncles and father could give as brujos. Without it, he was scared of what would happen. His body would feel sick, weak, and then it usually went all fuzzy then black, then red like the Big Red soda he liked to drink. Red like chamoy. Red like blood.

The older kids stuck together trying to think of ways to escape. They also watched out for the little ones. Some they didn't know, but still looked out for them. The girls were quiet because they were frightened by some of the guards and other strangers that walked around eyeing them up as if this place was a market stall.

No one told Chupa anything. It had been a few hours since he was given anything to drink.

The lights dimmed a little. He was so very tired. If only someone was there to sing him a song to sleep. He felt himself drifting away somewhere dark. It was going to be too late. Without the medicine he would be gone. The last thing he remembered was a man at the gated door waving him over.

The screams were heard across the camp. Terror radiated through the canvas walls like earthquake aftershocks. Men with guns ran around searching for the victim or victims of the atrocity that was occurring. All the lights turned on at once, waking those that had managed to get some sleep on the floor or foldaway cots.

Near an open delivery van lay a man with his throat and groin shredded to ground beef. Deep slashes cut through his face revealing bone and cartilage. The van was packed with cases of bottled water, but behind the water were toys, clothes, bags of sweets and a camera.

The officers continued their search, looking for open doors where the people were detained. Nothing was out of place. The lights stayed on the rest of the night.

Chupa waited behind a tree breathing heavily, feeling scared and angry. He was so angry that, if anyone bothered him again, he would do to them what he did to the man trying to drag him into the van.

A small frog leaped in front of his sight. Chupa grabbed the little thing before it could jump away ripped off its head in one bite. The frog went down nicely and Chupa buried his small seven-year-old body beneath fallen leaves. It was cool and comforting, like his mother's arms after a bad dream or when he didn't want to go to school. When it was night again, he would look for Mama and Papa.

When he awoke the camp was still busy and loud. He wanted the tall bright lights to go away so he could hide in the shadows and begin sniffing for their scent. It would be difficult because most of the people hadn't showered for days or brushed their teeth, children had accidents and the guards were slow to do anything about it. The toilets at the one end of the camp were overflowing and stank. Such a small place for so many of them.

Finally, it was quiet. Bedtime for everyone. He crept in the shadows, keeping away from where the children were. Mama and Papa wouldn't be there. Chupa was hungry again. The frog was but a small thing, a snack. Somewhere he could smell the grease of fried chicken and French fries. He loved both. A bag of food sat on a table just within reach. He didn't see anyone, so he scrambled to the table, pulling the bag down beneath a trailer. He ate the entire twelve-piece boneless meal in minutes. Satisfied from the first real sustenance in days, he would find his parents.

The scents were all muddled together. He was getting angry again, frustrated. His little body let out a whimper and a pained growl. There were too many of them. He scratched his head with his claws, trying to kick off the bugs caught in his fur. Where was Mama to wash them away? He curled up in a ball and began to cry. Then like a TV playing in another room, he heard her. It was her voice. Was she out of medicine, too? His pointy ears pricked up as her heartbeat grew louder. It was the same sound from before there was anything, when he floated and kicked for a way into the world until he finally gushed out in a waterfall of blood and white goo.

He scrambled to his feet, running through tent after tent looking for a way to Mama. He found her in the shower. She was crumpled in a ball, crying. Her eyes were puffy and as yellow as the sun before it goes to sleep again. She rose and let out a cry for him to come closer. She muzzled his fur as hers began to sprout. She fell to the floor once more, her body contorting and twisting. The filthy clothes on her back tore away.

She was still Mama. He was still Chupa. They let out a loud howl at the same time. Another call came back. It was Papa. They hopped to all fours, rushing past people and through canvas walls, overturning cots. People screamed, not knowing what was tearing through the fences. They didn't stop until they were well out of sight of the guards that didn't react quick enough to catch any of them anyway. Papa sat under a Pecan tree. They were together again, a family of Chupacabra. What they once thought to be a curse was now a gift—the gift of freedom. Together they howled in the night and returned home.

Cruz & Me

Oscar Mancinas

Two years ago we found a way in but still haven't found a way out. Even though I don't hear from Cruz every day, I still make the long trip to where we last saw each other. Where, before, I heard Cruz's voice, clear and recognizable. I sit and hear only the awful warble coming from nowhere. Cruz, te extraño, I want to say, but who or what am I even talking to?

wwwwwaaaaaaaaaaaaaaaaaaaaaaaaaaaaaaaaaaaatch

When Cruz first told me about the passage, I had nothing else to say except: What are we waiting for? Let's go!

Ever since we were kids, we loved going on adventures together, especially ones that got us out of our barrio and into parts of the city we didn't know. We were like explorers, we told ourselves—in a big, unknown world, but we made it back home to tell others of our discoveries and near-death experiences.

All right, for most of our lives we didn't have near-death experiences, or others to talk to about our adventures, but Cruz and me had each other, and that was enough for our adventures. It was.

ooooooooooooooooooooooooooouuuuuuuuuuuuuuuut

After walking for what felt like the whole afternoon, to the fringes of the valley where we lived, we finally got to where Cruz had seen it. Behind a Circle K, past some unpaved desert, was an old bridge over a dried-out canal tunnel. We had never been this far away from home, so I don't know how Cruz had found it, but when we went under the bridge, I saw it too.

It looked like a scar, a gash, like someone had torn open the air and ground underneath the bridge. The outside of the tear was fringed with red and blue sparks. The tear itself was bright, bright white, but it didn't make a sound and only gave off a faint light barely glowing on our dusty surroundings. For some reason, the white light didn't seem to touch our skin. We stood, shrouded in the cool darkness, staring at it.

Pretty crazy, right? Cruz said.

I heard the excitement, but I didn't share it. Instead, I felt a smoldering heat rise from my stomach up to my neck, face and ears. Cruz, I said, why are we here? Wh-what are we . . . why are we here?

Cruz put a hand on my shoulder, that's how I realized I was shaking.

Hey, hey, Cruz said. Cálmate. It's all good. I'm right here. Cruz's hand moved from one shoulder to the other, holding me. All the while, the scar was silent, unblinking.

I tried to breathe, to stop shaking. Who knows what I would've done if Cruz hadn't held me. And, at the same time, I could sense what Cruz was thinking. What had been our childhood together, going out and getting into mild trouble, stared at us as something I'm still not able to put into words. We weren't looking at the same thing.

Just as I went to say something, Cruz let me go, knelt to pick something up, and then threw whatever it was into the gash.

Nothing.

See? Cruz said. It ain't a big deal, you know? I've even stuck like a hand and foot into it before, and it doesn't really feel like anything, just . . . like, slightly warmer or, like, cleaner . . . you know? Kinda like here but maybe a little less contaminated by pollution or something. I don't know, but. . . .

That brought me back. What the fuck are you talking about, Cruz? I finally said, turning to look down at where Cruz knelt.

Cruz sighed but didn't look up.

Cruz, I said. You found something weird, all right? And, yeah, it's interesting, I guess, but we need to just leave it alone, okay? I'm sorry I just yelled, but we should get—

What're you so afraid of? Cruz said, standing and looking at me for the first time since we'd arrived. I didn't bring you here to freak you out, you know? Like, Cruz sighed again, I wanted to show you this because we share things, we . . . like, do things together, no?

I didn't know what to say. In my silence, Cruz, took a few steps away from me, toward the white tear, turned back to look at me, and said, So are we doing this together, or am I doing this alone?

sssssssstttttttaaaaaaaaaaaaaaaaaaaaaaaaaaaaaaay

Here you might expect me to tell you we fought like that all the time, that we had our issues, that Cruz left because we'd been on separate paths for a while. I don't say this to call you out or to judge; I grew up with these kinds of stories from my tías and tíos, from mis abuelos, from my cousins. Things get bad in one of two ways without us noticing. Either they simmer, slowly, smoldering in the background of brighter, louder problems in need of immediate attention; or they explode before we get a chance to brace ourselves. It's not a question of if, but when, and for how long.

That wasn't us.

Cruz and me had something special. From the time we were kids until we both grew up, we'd shared something beyond any word or action. One of the few fights we ever had was over what was or wasn't a horror movie.

Cruz started by saying, Alright, so if you had to pick your favorite horror movie, you would say. . . .

Um, *Silence of the Lambs*, I think?

Cruz and me loved movies, we loved to watch them, talk about them, disagree about them, dream about maybe making a movie together someday.

No, no, no. You gotta pick something else.

What? Why? It's a scary movie!

So? Scary don't equal "horror." You're talking about how something makes you feel, I'm talking about, like, a type of movie with specific elements. *Silence of the Lambs* is scary, no doubt, but it's, like, a psychological thriller, not a horror movie.

Oh, so you're an expert now, huh? Chief Justice of the Criterion Channel court, qué no? I tried to laugh, but Cruz was serious.

I just want us on the same page. Like, I'm talking about stories that start with everything mostly seeming normal, we meet an average person who doesn't realize what they're about to be dragged through because they don't know they're a character in something outside of their control. Clarice Starling's already an FBI trainee, she's got training, she's got a gun and she's, rightly, suspicious of almost every man she meets in her line of work. She's got things to face, but she can mostly handle them.

I just nodded. My face and neck were getting hot.

You know what I mean? Like, a for-real horror movie is, like, the OG *Halloween*. Laurie Strode isn't built to handle what Carpenter's about to put her through. To me, that's like a good way to think about horror. A person realizing they're gonna be put through a nightmare and also realizing they can't do a damn thing about it, except survive, because they don't get a choice. They're not the authors of their own destinies. Laurie's trapped in a world where she has no alternative but to keep going, keep trying to live.

Neither of us spoke for a minute. We sat there, looking ahead at the blank TV screen in front of us, and hearing the sounds of birds and people out on the streets.

Finally, I calmed myself and said, All right, then, what's your favorite horror movie?

Cruz was silent, looking away from me. I started to feel myself getting hot again. What was the point of having such a random, rigid set of rules for something that didn't matter outside of us? Was Cruz just trying to make me feel dumb?

Probably . . . either *Halloween* or *The Texas Chainsaw Massacre*, because I think they're both scary in a quiet, isolating kinda way, you know? Like, the monsters are in your neighborhood or hiding along empty, country roads. If home isn't safe but the open road isn't either, where are you supposed to go? Where can you run to, you know?

Cruz turned to me, smiled.

I nodded, said nothing.

After a moment, though, Cruz spoke again. But if we wanna expand our terms, and you say *Silence of the Lambs*, then I'd also consider *Tésis* by Alejandro Amenábar. Ángela knows she's pursuing something she shouldn't, both in guys she's attracted to and her thesis on ultraviolent movies and media, but she can't stop herself. She has to follow that path even as she realizes how much danger she's putting herself in; like she's her own writer, going deeper into where the monsters in her mind live. It's got a cool, like, meta thing, doesn't it?

Yeah, Cruz. Whatever you say, I said. I stood up and walked out the room.

aaaaaaaaaaaaaaaaaaaaaaaawwwwwwaaaaaaaaaaaaaaay

We didn't talk much about it after that. We tied a rope around Cruz's skinny waist and I took the other end. We gave each other one last, reassuring look. Cruz stepped into the opening.

Nothing.

I watched. Even within the tear, Cruz still seemed untouched by any of it. All of Cruz's movements still looked as though they were part of this world and not another.

Then Cruz turned around and smiled. Suddenly, the smile locked. Cruz's dark, brown pupils vanished, and what was left of the eyes began to bubble and leak like milk boiling in an overloaded pot. Then, Cruz's the teeth, their pattern of beige and ivory separated by vacuous black, spread down Cruz's neck, silhouetting the body to the feet and fingernails.

I only saw Cruz like that for a second. Then the tear sealed itself, severing the rope clean.

I was alone.

I don't know how long I stood beneath that bridge, motionless, barely breathing, but all I could do was stare at where I'd last seen Cruz, think about how I'd last seen Cruz.

Cruz? I felt myself whisper. Then, louder, Cruz? Cruz? Cruz? Louder still, Cruz?!

I was about to turn and leave, go for help, but then I heard:

I'm here. I'm here. Here. Don't. Don't . . .

I looked around, saw nothing. Cruz? I said, whe-where are you?

I don't know. I don't know. I don't. I don't know . . .

The voice sounded like it was coming through a metal tube or an old, worn speaker.

I. I can't really say. Say. I. Can't really say. Say. Oh. Oh. Wait. Wait. I. I. Think. I think I see. See something. Something. Like. Like. A road, yeah. Yeah. Wait. Wait . . .

What? What, Cruz? What do you see? Where are you? I said.

I-I'm. I-I'm not. Not too. Not too far from. From You. You. Too far.

Cruz? I said. Please try not to go too far. Please . . . please try to stay, Cruz. Cruz, please come back . . .

I sank to the ground and hugged my knees to my face. Cruz. I sobbed.

Waaaaaaaiiiiiit, wwwaaaaaaaaiiiiiiit.

I'm not sure if Cruz can hear me, if Cruz can see me, if Cruz knows when I'm beneath the bridge or when I'm home or when I'm at one of my jobs, keeping my mind busy and myself supported. I don't know.

I don't know how long it took before I realized the tear wasn't going to reopen. I keep coming back to this spot, half-afraid I'll never see Cruz again and half-afraid I will and it'll be the same image of Cruz I saw last. Sometimes I still call out Cruz's name, hoping I'll hear mine called in return. I've thought about giving up, about letting go of Cruz completely. Without Cruz, the Cruz I knew before the tear, do I have any control over my destiny? But then I think that thoughts like these—the ones that give me reasons to keep coming back—

have become some of the last glowing embers I have of Cruz.
What else am I supposed to think? What more can I say?
helllllllllllllllllllllllllllllllllllllllllllllllllllllllllllllllllllllllllllllllllllllllllllllllllp

It Said "Bellevue"

Sydney Macias

1

"I haven't been dead for very long," she told them. Mari took the needle from their patient's stiff pale arm, adjusted and took a fifth jab at the woman's veins. She didn't flinch since she could no longer feel her body. We were just taking up her newfound eternity.

Mary-Anne Demoure was a new transfer to this unit. When she sat up straight in the morgue, having died from an egregious amount of happy pills, the autopsy technician immediately fainted. One frantic phone call later had someone from the secret depths of Bellevue Hospital rushing to collect her graying form. Now she sat in bed seven of the Humanoid Unit, complaining about how we attempted to reanimate her.

Mari shot me a burning look of annoyance as Mary-Anne turned to primp her curled blonde hair with her free hand.

"Sorry, Mrs. Demoure. Rigor mortis is a hard state to get around, but lucky for you now there's all the time in the world. We'll get those fluids in soon and hopefully we can have you home by the end of the week."

"End of the week!" Mary-Anne shot upright causing Mari to miss the vein a sixth time. I put on a thin smile.

"There are certain rehabilitation stages before we allow the Undead to go back into the world." Mary-Anne huffed. If her blood had been pumping, I could imagine redness blotting her thin face. "Some clients never get to go back to their old homes, or lives. You're in a special group." My voice lilted up with mock excitement. *Remember your place*, stuck on my tongue.

Mari stopped dancing around polite procedure and dug the needle deeply into our patient. Mrs. Demoure didn't notice, her eyes bore into me. I had to admit, she was probably just as terrifying in life. This kind of woman always got what she wanted, because who could possibly deny her dreams? Mrs. Demoure was one of the most intimidating creatures we had this week.

Sure, there was the woman in bed two who was perpetually soaked in murky water, dirtied streams coming from her every orifice. There was the eight-foot-tall man, whose neck made up two feet of that height, with arms long enough to drag his knuckles across the floor. I did hate the porcelain child, with his cracked face showing the hollow body some spirit had made home. They were all scary, but the worst was always the patients so close to life.

Especially to the living and breathing staff who had been plucked from normal practices. I've been here less than a year, I still remember what it is to treat actual people, to practice real medicine and to work in the daylight. Treating Mary-Anne felt like a rare glimpse back into everything I used to want for myself. She was also a reminder that those dreams were lost. I could never return to the waking world with all I've learned about the Underground. Of course, this is exactly why I was transferred here. So that people *up there* didn't have to make room for me.

2

Bellevue Hospital has always been a Nexus of medical achievement. It attracts people from all over the world to get the best care. Bellevue has seen every kind of patient you could possibly imagine, and the ones you couldn't.

Growing up so near to this illustrious institution, I was drawn to its magic. For as long as I can remember, I have pictured myself walking Bellevue's halls, becoming part of the legend itself. Between nursing school and working for a doctorate, I sent out only one application. My future was in Bellevue. I thought I knew everything about this place. Yet, it was far more extraordinary than I expected.

Tucked away in the Old Campus, where the shimmering glass towers gave away to rust colored colonial structures, a squat brick and mortar building stands unnoticed. The ancient hospital wings surround it, three stories high with faded and fogged windows.

There's a little building in the corner, with two white double doors, that was said to house the hospital's staff in the late eighteenth century all the way up through the twentieth. It was kept prim and proper with beds that appeared to have never been slept in. A small time capsule, mere historical attraction, and an easy opportunity for misdirection. For this was home to Bellevue Hospital's most experimental and terrifying wings.

Hidden behind false kitchen shelves, the building's real purpose lurked. Listen carefully and the metal whirring of a freight elevator can be heard. It was a large gray space. There was no need to make it look proper like the elevators in the new wings. No music played and the walls weren't nicely designed or cleaned.

No, this elevator didn't hide what it was. The deep scratches in the metal, dent and holes, stains that wouldn't come out told you exactly what was in store as it descended to the lower levels. This was a portal to the Underworld. Or, as we call it, the Underground. A little less terrifying this way.

My name is Nola Castro and I've been nursing creatures and phantoms of myth down here for six months. So unlike many of my coworkers, I didn't happen upon an otherworldly *thing*, I didn't find the secret door to this unit or have a natural born second sight for the supernatural. But I ended up here nonetheless.

This month my team has been moved to one of our more unsettling units. When I first arrived, the most terrifying shifts came with caring for beasts and true monsters of the night. Large, and growling, they were the rude awakening into realizing another world lived parallel to ours. However, today I would rather work with some foul-smelling wild dog who bares its fangs at anything warm-blooded and tasty than a patient who spoke back.

3

Mari pulls Mary-Anne's door shut with fervor. She tips her forehead against the thick metal, scrunching her dark bangs up. I can't stop the smile that turns my lips up.

"I swear to god, I'm going to fill her with embalming fluid and call it a day." Now I really laugh. "What?" Mari continues, "Those used to be the rules right? You died, then you got preserved and buried. Actually, that's kind of weird if you think about it."

"More weird than dying and waking back up to an eternal life?" Mari squints at me like she's weighing the options fairly. She has been down here for years. I guess the two worlds are more equal in her eyes. Instead of answering properly, Mari signs and walks over to the nurses station. Of course, the desk sat empty.

"Where would Jackson be today?" I ask after the assigned attending.

"Smoke break? Nap break? I don't think he really works here yet." With only two months under his belt, the poor guy tries to spend as little time as possible down here. It takes some longer than others to wrap their minds around this life.

As if on cue, the familiar metal whirring of our elevator pursed from down the hall. I understand needing to get out of this place for a bit, but it's technically against the rules to leave so often. We don't want to draw attention to an apparently empty building.

Waiting to see the uneasiness on Jackson's face as he walks back into the fray, I peer down the brightly lit hall. The wings down here were designed to simulate daylight. Or more accurately, the absence of night. Though it's just as scary to see otherworldly creatures in full light as it would be in pure darkness. Mari rustles up a pink box from below the desk.

"*Concha?*" She lifts a small round bread with a pink sugared top that makes the treat look like a seashell.

"Is that what these are called?" I reach over to take a piece. "What do you call them?"

"*Pan dulce.* It's what my nana always said." Mari shrugs as if to accept this.

Finally, the thick metal doors open to reveal a hunched over Jackson. Something is wrong, I can feel it.

"Nola?" Mari calls after me, as I start to run down the hall.

Jackson is trembling. And he is holding up a body. At first, it looks like one dark arm is slung over the nurse, but then it starts to take shape. Jackson slides it out from the elevator just before it falls from his grip, collapsing to the tiled floors.

One moment it is small, dark and thin like a shadow, the next it grows and swells in places. Patches of it become skin-like, dark and pock-marked. It looks like it is stuck between different forms, trying to become whole. It groans in pain.

"I don't know," Jackson starts in a panic, "I don't know what it is!" Frankly, neither did I. He wrings his hands together over and over, almost unsure if he should try and touch it again.

"What happened?"

"I was walking back from my break." He throws up his arms in exasperation and gestures down to the thing. "It just appeared in front of me. It spoke. It can speak. It said *Bellevue*."

4

Our new patient waits in room ten, a shapeless shadow on the bed. I watch it from a security camera, the display screen posted next to the door. Since we laid it down, the thing has been perfectly still. I remotely dim the overhead lights of the room. As suspected, the shadow doesn't change. It wasn't formed by light, nor holds the rules of it.

Mari had no idea what we were dealing with here. Jackson told us the *thing* appeared to him as it was now, a silhouette with no attempt at imitating a human form. Mari suspects the creature becomes more unstable depending on the number of people who see it. It is possible that it tried to subconsciously morph itself to look like us for its own protection.

"What are you waiting for?" Mari asks over my shoulder. I suppress the shiver down my spine. You'd think that someone who works around such terrifying things would be more careful about sneaking up on others. Our uniform shoes are partly to blame. Their nature is to be soundless, as to keep us hidden if any hostile creature got loose.

I still shoot her a soft glare before looking down to the tray in my hand. It is a hot mess of standard medical instruments for testing and analysis, along with our secretly developed tools to gage a creature's energy and toxicity. The sensors built into the room show that, whatever it is, doesn't irradiate the air or open unnatural energy pockets. With a firm hand and an all-too-comfortable mask of calm, I open the room's steel door with a hiss.

The creature immediately bolts upright. What appears to be its head turns to me, but looks straight at Mari, who's still looking in from behind me. The center of the head opens up in a scream. Where the sound comes from, I couldn't say, but the shadow peels back in pain. It starts to become more three dimensional. I can make out arms and skin, maybe hair.

"Don't worry," I rush to close Mari out, "I'm the only one coming in. It's just me." My patient's metamorphosis slows. Instead of a flurry of growing and shaping, the shadow drifts lightly into a human outline. It bulks up, filling out to no longer be between shadow and body. It looks down at itself as if also wondering what it will become.

When it's solid, I see an aging man with brown skin that's dotted with sun marks. Its bones are just a little too long in some places, a little too big or slim so it appears unproportional. Yet it is human.

"You know, you don't have to look like this for us, we know you're . . . something else. What we saw out there, was that you? The shadow." I set my tools at its bedside.

"No, that wasn't right." Its voice is deep and vibrating. It flows out like wind. "It hurt." Its eyes are glazed and its dry lips tremble with each word. I think of giving it water, but can it drink?

"Is it easier to show yourself to just one person?" Mari's theory was proving true.

"It is easier to show myself to you." It looks up at me with dark round eyes and makes no move to change its form.

"You're still looking awfully human."

"Well, of course." It smiles with those cracking lips. "What else would I be?"

5

I smile at the thing that cannot be a man.

"You said it hurts to try to look this way. Is that all that brought you in today?" It looks corporeal enough at this point, so I move to start my standard tests. Only, just as I reach out, the thing pulls away.

"It only hurts for others to look. I'm alright now, I came to help," it says with the voice that buzzes through my chest as if I were standing near a loudspeaker.

"Help who?"

"*Mi hija*, she's lost. I came to help," it repeats. The haze in its eyes has been clearing, but they fill again with something that makes me look away.

"You think she's here? We don't have any—" I don't have a word for this creature yet. "We don't have anything else like you." But it came straight here, I think. It came to us, to Bellevue. It couldn't possibly mean any other wing, could it? It looks confused, pulling the man's eyebrows together and wrinkling the forehead.

"What am I?"

"I was going to ask *you* that." I almost want to laugh. "You can't be both human and shadow. Plus, you came here. There aren't supposed to be people here."

"You're here. Are you not a person?" Its voice still thrums through me, but softer now.

"You're right, but I'm a nurse. I have to be here to help things like you." The thing shakes its head. I forward with my testing, first with the tools I would use for a human so I can find out how far this transformation goes.

"*M'ija* is a doctor." At this, I do laugh. Something in my chest tightens but I speak anyway. I don't know why.

"I was going to be a doctor. I studied for it. Got really close, too." He smiles at me—it, it smiles at me.

"What happened, *m'ija*?" I stop halfway through taking off the blood pressure cuff. For its part, the device gives no reading. Its voice is nothing like I've ever heard but he calls me *m'ija,* and somewhere in my past I hear my nana call to me.

The thing watches me. I clear my throat and start unpacking a needle set.

"What always happens to us—" and I'm surprised to hear myself say it. I'm surprised to admit how I got here. "There are enough women upstairs. Enough Castros," I say like this thing will know what I mean. "They sent me here, ya know, *where I'm needed*." I sit forward to prep the injection site, but the thing closes a hand over mine. Through the blue latex gloves I feel its weight, its warmth.

"You say you have to be here, in this place people shouldn't be?"

"I misspoke. I meant humans don't get treated here, but someone does have to work for you." My mouth tastes bitter, I think my soul does too.

"You also say I am not human when I am." It shakes its head again. "You see? You're lost, *m'ija*. I have felt it."

6

"I'm sorry, I can't be who you're looking for." Sympathy swells inside me. This is why humanoids are so dangerous. I can't let myself forget that this is an *it* and not a *him*. It might be some kind of spirit. "And you don't appear to be human, at least not anymore. I promise we'll try to help you. You might be the one who's lost." It smiles.

"I know what I am. I am an Old One.

"Far, far gone from you. But I heard *m'ija* was lost.

"She didn't know what she was. She forgets.

"Her familia watches over her, but none were as strong as me.

"None could come walking. None could show her the way."

"What way was that?" My voice is a whisper.

"That it is possible to be more than one thing. It's possible to be all things. You say I'm not human and I can't argue that what you have seen isn't human. No, when I came here I became something new to myself. But before this . . ." it gestures to the form that can't be real, ". . . I was human. That won't go away. I was a man, so here I appear as one." Its eyes narrow at me. "Just like all the work you put into being a doctor. You'll never lose that." My eyes start to burn, but I blink back everything that's rising to the surface.

"I'm afraid what I know doesn't count for much anymore. I never got my degree, so I'm just *almost* something." A sentiment I have known for a long time.

Top of the class, *almost.* American, a*lmost.* Mexican, *almost.* A doctor . . .

Almost. Almost. Almost.

"I see. You think there are spaces in between." A small, irritable flame lights in my chest.

"I can't call myself something I'm not."

"You can't deny the work you've done either. Can't ignore how you *do* fit in certain places. It might not be the way you want, or the way other people think you should, but you fit.

"You have every right to be up there, or down here, whichever you actually choose.

"I came to show you the truth, *m'ija*.

"That you are all things.

"None of them are wrong, or not enough. You are enough.

"You think you belong to nothing, but you belong to everything."

He smiles again and I feel the sun on my skin. I feel the warmth of the day, even way down here.

What the Hurricane Took

Ann Dávila Cardinal

Sandra? Hello? Sandra?

Oh my God—

Are you there? Sandra?

I'm here . . . can't . . . manage . . . for it!

Oh, you're breaking up! Now all I hear is the wind. Shit! Shit! Are you okay?

[Crackling line]

Are you in the middle of the storm? Are you okay?

I'm okay! Luisa and I are sheltering . . . bathroom with . . . dogs.

Oh, thank God! I wasn't sure whether she was with you or in Ponce.

I'm so glad you're together. How is the rest of the family?

I haven't been able to get in touch with them either. Aren't the phones down?

Not . . .

. . . Sandra? Oh shit. I think I lost you. I wish I could talk with you. If you can still hear me, stay safe, *prima!* I love you. . . .

H-hello? Sandra? Is that you? *¡Gracias a Dios!* I'm so glad to hear from you!

I've been trying to reach you all day! I'm glad I could finally get through.

I'm just so happy to hear your voice. . . . How are you?

Oh, okay. We did better than most since we had shelter and a generator.

And the rest of the family? Everyone safe?

I think I checked on everyone. They're okay; as best as can be expected, I suppose.

As you can imagine, Tío is in his glory.

Ha! Yeah, he's been working toward this for fifty years! He was a prepper before that became a thing.

Yeah, but you got to question all those years we mocked him for his battery, flashlight and cash hoarding. I mean, right now he's the only one who can buy things since the ATH machines are down. He's buying propane for his whole block.

I love that man.

I gotta go, *prima*, I only have a bit of charge left and I have to call my partners at the firm. We have to figure out how we're going to get through this.

Okay, thanks for calling! And Sandra?

Hmm?

I'm really, really glad you're okay.

Me too, love you!

Miss me, *prima*?

Yeah, I just wanted to check in on you this morning. You're the only family member I seem to be able to reach. Jesus, Sandra! What are those dogs doing? Sounds like a kennel!

Oh, they've probably found some more rats in the courtyard.

What? You have rats?

Yeah, they came up from the sewers like an invading army after they flooded. Now they're running through the neighborhood. The dogs have caught four already.

Really? What do they do with them . . . wait, don't tell me. I don't want to know.

We all gotta eat.

Eww! So, other than your savage dogs, how are you holding up?

Oh, I'm okay. Better than most down here. After hurricane Irma Tío set me up with a generator and it kicks in as needed. You should see the neighborhood. It's so dark here at night without street and traffic lights. It's kind of nice.

Kind of like Vermont all the time.

Yeah, but without the ridiculous cold!

Hey, it's a balmy fifty here today!

Shudder!

That's work calling. Please keep me posted. I'm worried about you.

Will do, I promise. *Besos!*

Sandra? Is that you? Are you okay?

Yeah, I'm just . . . it just . . . hit me.

Oh. I've been surprised at how calm you've seemed. I would have been sucking my thumb in the corner, rocking back and forth from day one.

I'd like to, believe me. But what good would that do?

Are you kidding? A lot of good! I like to totally freak out at least every couple of months. Keeps my skills sharp.

Thank you. I needed a laugh today.

What's going on?

I don't know. I'm a few blocks away from my house, standing outside this small family business in my neighborhood. I've been watching them put up early Christmas decorations, as if they are still going to be in business by then. It's just making me so sad.

Oh, Sandra, I'm so sorry.

No, I'm sorry. You don't want to sit there and listen to me cry from two thousand miles away. Really, I'm okay.

Please don't apologize. I just wish there was something I could do. I tried to book a flight but since the airport is basically closed, they couldn't sell me a ticket.

Ha! Tío would kill you. You're the one member of his flock he knows is safe and sound.

I know, I can imagine how pissed he'd be. I just wish I could talk to him on the phone. I don't know why I can't reach him. You're sure he's okay?

Yes, yes. He was at my house today, in fact.

He's always so concerned about me since I live alone.

Yeah, I get that. Oh! Do I hear *coquís?*

Yes, poor things. Their population was pretty decimated after the hurricane, but they're hardy little buggers!

That sound . . . so comforting. I'm surprised to hear them in the shopping district.

Shopping district? I'm home on the patio.

What? I thought you said you were outside a store. I didn't hear your car while we were talking.

True. I . . . must have walked.

Wait, *must have?* Don't you remember?

Oh *prima*, you have to stop worrying about us. We're fine!

Okay . . . I just don't understand.

Join the club. I don't understand anything anymore. Love you!

Tío? Is that you? God, Tío it's so good to hear your voice. How did you get through? I've been trying to reach you for days!

I know, *sobrina*, I'm sorry to worry you. But the cell towers have been down since the first night of the storm. And I've been very busy trying to help out our neighbors.

I know! I heard. You buying propane for the entire community?

You heard? How could you have heard, *querida?*

Oh, Tío, you know me. I have spies everywhere! How's Titi? Is she working around the clock at the hospital?

Yes, she is working very hard. You know your aunt. But *sobrina*, I wanted to make sure you knew.

Knew what? Wait, I don't like the sound of your voice. What's wrong?

It's Sandra. . . .

What? No, don't scare me like that. I just talked to her an hour ago.

I'm afraid that's not possible. . . . Is everything okay, *m'ija?*

Sure, I'm fine. What happened with Sandra?

It was the first night of the storm. A tree, it fell on her house and crushed the roof right over the bathroom where they were sheltering. They were able to get Luisa out, but I'm afraid *pobre* Sandra was killed instantly.

No . . . no, that's not possible.

I know, it is hard to accept, we all loved her so much. But she is with God now.

No, Tío, I mean it's literally not possible. I've talked to Sandra three times since the hurricane. She called me three times, and I called her—

Querida . . . there have been no phones, and Sandra . . . well, I identified her body yesterday.

I don't understand. We talked about the dogs eating rats, and—

Yes, I found the dogs today. They survived well taking care of the neighborhood rat problem, but I'm afraid there is no way you spoke to Sandra.

You worry so much it's made you imagine things. How—

I'm not imagining anything, I . . . wait . . . I have a call coming in from Puerto Rico, it's. . . .

I—oh . . . um, Tío, you're absolutely right, I've just been so worried . . . let me call you back in twenty minutes, okay?

All right, *sobrina*, but—

Hello? Sandra?

TAMALES

José Alaniz

2063

El cohete, bent and broken on the Martian sands, orange sands. Strewn eggshells of hull, arced over the horizon. The red sun, wan, sunken, in a pink nest of clouds. The dead ship's jagged shadows. A darkening sky. Slowly darkening. The howls of distant sandstorms, the air, thin air, filled with their hollow drone. The eyes of stars, winking open.

A campfire, fed with rags and cohete offal by the old woman perched on a gray trunk nearby. Her head bent over the flat top of a crate, quivering lightly to the rhythm of her hands. A small mole on her cheek lit up by the lick of the flames, eyes silent and intent. Yellow dough taking shape before her. The movements of her hands, quick, youthful, the dough stretched and flattened into a gooey mass, breathing. A rich corn smell. The husks on another battered trunk, beside her, covered with a strip of cloth slowly gathering dust. The woman's expression, flat and featureless as the desert sprawl, in every direction, to forever. The moan of the wind, a lulling calm. The fire's halo.

"It's done," said the old man, gruffly, descending the crest of a rise. He climbed over cables spilled out of the *cohete* like seaweed. He picked up the long snake of wires baled together, looked up to the cohete, as if to stuff the tangled strands back into its dark maw. He took a few wobbly steps, when his gaze fell on a small object tangled in the wires—a doll, in a little pink dress. Smiling with rosy cheeks. The old man set the cables down again, angrily, and walked on. Each heavy step kicked up puffs of Martian sand, thin puffs. The wind slowly whittled them down to nothing.

"Didn't you hear me? I'm done. It's finished." The old man stood before the fire, removed his cream-colored hat, its inside splotchy with sweat stains. He wiped his brow. "Fucking dust."

The flame's wavering light slid over his face like water as he pounded out sparse orange clouds from his clothes. His tall, lanky body resembled a skeleton: his skin, the texture of rock, stretched tight over the bones, the skull's shape sharp against the purpling sky. The old man scratched his bald head with a sinewy arm. Gazed absently at a mound of disturbed earth several yards away. Replaced his hat. Without his hat he looked and felt unlike himself. Spat. The fire crackled, just audible above the wind.

He turned to his wife. "What are you doing?" He saw. "I told you you're wasting your time, woman. That storm is coming tonight. Can't you hear it? Are you deaf? By morning everything here will be buried twenty feet deep in sand. Us too. Are you listening to me? Are you listening? I said we'll be dead. We'll be dead by the time you finish your goddamn tamales. The storm is coming and we'll be dead, you stupid old. . . . Didn't you hear? Forget that. I told you anyway I'm not hungry. There's no time for that. Forget it. No hay tiempo."

Amparo stands beside the grave, stiff and erect, as her grandson snaps one picture after another. The December day is cool but half-sunny; she wears her sweater unbuttoned. She is seventy-three. The grass over-green with juice, freshly mowed. The flowers on the headstone, perfectly arranged. A flawed petal, plucked away, her quick gesture of a bird. As the camera clicks and the grandson shifts positions around her, Amparo adjusts the kerchief over her ears against the wind, lowers her passive, stony face over the immaculate mound.

El cohete sailing smoothly through the dark, its engine's powerful hum perceptible in the black throttle, feeling good in his hands, the distant red orb growing like a spill as he falls, falls towards it, a perfect shot, to the future, the future, to streets he himself will pave with gold. . . .

"Come here," he says. The boy starts timidly at the sound. The boy lies in the corner under a sheet, his head on his mother's stomach, his eyes open, with the women, trembling. A skinny thing cringing in the dark.

"I said come here!"

The boy hesitates, sees his mother and sisters asleep, then crawls, quivering, across the metal deck, through the hatch, into the tiny cockpit with its dim blinking lights and black oval porthole. . . . It's so cold in the cohete that the boy's flesh contracts, shrinks, his puny body trying to escape into itself. . . .

"Take it. Take it," I said. "Come on. No es nada. *No es nada.*"

The boy takes the throttle, his hand pulled over onto it by a stronger, surer grasp . . . the instrument shakes so violently in his clutch, he has to hold on tight to keep from flying off, he presses down on the round black knob with all his meager weight, the cohete pours its wild, surging power into his body, the boy rattles, crying out feebly as the old man laughs, laughs, his breath fogging up the porthole. . . .

"That's it! Ha ha! Hold on to it, boy! You're in control now. Keep it steady," I said. "You're in control now. Don't let go, or you'll spin us out into the dark. Don't let go, te digo. You want to kill us all before we even get there? Hold on. You're a man now. You're a man. No es nada," I said. "No es nada . . ."

The old man cursed and shouted, kicked at the crushed metal box he'd dragged out of the *cohete*. He had pried the box open with a strip of the hull's lining he'd crudely bent into an instrument. The makeshift bar bit into his hand. Drops of blood fell onto the sand, Martian sand. Sucked it up greedily. He yelled at the old woman, a string of threats and complaints leveled at her back, her back in silhouette against the fire.

The fire, dying out, fed with scraps of clothing. Pallid smoke, pinkish flame, choked, suffocated in the thin air. No moon on Mars, not even a crescent. But familiar. The desert, familiar. The sand, wind, stars, the same. The flame weak, the stars misty, but the light just enough. Just enough to work by. Dough in her hands, soft and moist, like flesh, corn flesh, rolled around in the bowl, pressed up under her fingernails. The bowl covered with a rag, protected from the sand. Escaped sounds, smells of kneaded dough from inside the bowl, under the rag. The rag from clothing. Women's clothing. A dress. A pile of women's clothing beside her, to feed the fire. A lot of women's clothing now. Girl's clothing.

He stopped up the gash's flow with a pañuelito; a shallow wound, red gleaming, fresh against his skin's orange pallor. His hand bandaged, the old man turned to the box. A transparent liquid flowed out of it, joined his blood on the ground, sunk quickly into the parched earth. A penetrating stench rose from the box, along with fizzing noises.

"Fuck, fuck, fuck," he grumbled, reaching into the container with his good hand, moving something around inside. In the end, he found only one bottle intact.

He wiped it off on his shirt. The old man uncapped it and took a long swig, his elbow pointed straight up at the sky. His throat pulsed beneath the skin like some animal. He took the dark bottle from his mouth, ran his tongue along the inside of his cheeks, licked his lips. He did this twice. He then walked over to a point just beneath the cohete's nose. It towered at an angle some thirty feet up from the sand, from where the ship had half-buried itself on impact. He took off his hat. Put it down on a crate. He took out his cigarettes from his shirt pocket, lit one up with an electric lighter. The sun, dull red, snuffed itself out on the wispy horizon. The old man smoked and drank silently, a vacant expression. He stared before him at a small crater in the earth, slowly filling with a film of windborne sand.

The clinic smells of sterile alcohol mixed with urine. Next to Cruz's bed, behind a thin white curtain, lies a man who lost a leg in World War II. The stump, uncovered, is knobbed and obscenely erect. The man watches television with no sound and the empty eyes of a statue. Cruz squirms in his soiled sheets, rumpled like paper. The tongue, an independent thing, glides over his lips, inside his mouth, incessantly. The grandson zooms the camcorder into Cruz's face, its two tiny eyes that seem to have no whites. His hands like claws, like a vulture's or some other carrion bird's; the nurses have put red rubber balls in his palms to keep his fingers from clenching, getting stiff, as if keep-

ing the fingers apart will keep him alive. A tube goes from a slit in his stomach to the suspended placental drip bag that feeds him a white slop. The wisp of hair on his egg-shaped head, the vulture claws, the fetal posture: like some newborn chick, helpless, hairless, awaiting the flutter of its mother's wing, mumbling chirps in a nest of wrinkles. He is 87. His diaper needs changing. Amparo tells her grandson to put his toy down and help her turn him over. He utters vague noises of complaint as he is pushed and pulled and the sheets are replaced, first one side, then the other. Ya, ya, ya, Amparo tells him.

~ ~ ~

Goddamn cocksucking motherfuckers, those bastard coyotes, those fuckers, they told him, they told him the *cohete* worked, the goddamn cohete would get them there, those fucking hijos de puta, those cocksuckers, those coyotes took their money, a wife and nine kids, but hey, hermano, it's okay, we understand you want to bring them, yeah, bring them over, it's lonely out there, we understand, hermano, fuck you fuck you, everybody's crossing with wives and kids and chickens y todo el chingadero, they're all coming, hermano, those fucking cockroaches called him hermano, yes, fuck you coyotes fuck you and they took his money, yes, and they gave him a goddamn motherfucking piece of shit *cohete* that explodes halfway to the other side, those bastards los mato a esos coyotes los mato los mato and el cohete is spinning and steam is blowing out everywhere and alarms are screaming and the girls are screaming and the gravity's gone and bodies are flying and something's burning, it's all burning. . . .

"Come on, woman!" le grita el viejo, gives her his hand in the mad tumble of hair and arms and legs and luggage and equipment, he holds the boy up against him in the tiny emergency pod designed for one, un cohete designed for six, a cohete stuffed with eleven bodies, those cocksucking coyote fuckers, he holds out his hand and screams at her, the boy screams for her, a thousand different sounds boom and toss them in the dark inside the twisting cohete gone insane. . . .

"Come on!" He grabs his wife by the hair, by the neck, by the arm, pulls her floating round body into the pod like a bloated balloon, she kicks her feet, struggling, grabs hold of something, her flesh pressed up against them, filling the pod, the warmth of her body, the veins pulsing, engorged, the pod crammed, the boy's puke swimming in bubbles through the air, the hiss of emergency oxygen through the vents, he gropes, blind, for the handle. . . .

"Get back! No! No room! Get back!" the old man yells, the face of his daughter in the hatch, his daughter, the youngest, barely older than the boy, his daughter and her seven sisters in the cohete's hold, they're choking, burning, slammed against the walls, a hole in the wall, the rush of air bursting out, metal flying, he must close the hatch, la niña screams, cries, begs him, begs him please papi please papi, holds onto the hatch with a tiny brown hand, begging him, but he's caught the handle, he has it he pulls it, he swings the hatch towards the lock, the hatch crushes the little hand, he slams it, the locks engage, the pod is sealed, the three of them are in. Outside the sounds are no longer human and the hatch secure and only then does the old woman understand, only then does she react: she screams no, no, no, no, no, her scream louder and louder and louder, no, no, no until her scream fills everything, until the pod becomes her scream.

Fuck you coyotes fuck you fuck you los mato los mato los mato a todos los mato shut up shut up fuck you coyotes I'll come back and kill you you're dead you're fucking dead fuck you fuckyoucocksuckersyou'redeadyou'realldeadmotherfuck ersss.

⁂

Tamales.

Tamales de carne. Tamales de res. Tamales de puerco. Tamales de frijoles. And the boy's favorite, tamales de azúcar. The nimble work of her hands, their smooth, quick movements, a pinch of raisins poured in each flattened mound of dough, each then folded up and wrapped in a corn husk.

Tamales de pasitas, the boy called them, waiting wide-eyed at the table. A moustache of hot chocolate over his lip. His favorite.

⁂

Déjalo morir. Es Dios que lo quiere. Por eso lo hace enfermo. Porque ya lo quiere, que venga ya, que es tiempo ya. ¿Por qué no lo dejas ir? She makes no answer. She stares at him. On her face is no discernible emotion. She stares at him, lying on the reclining bed. Another hospital. Working his tongue. He is eighty-five. She stares at him. She makes no answer.

⁂

"No. No. No se arrimen."

El viejo mumbles in his sleep, turns over angrily. Scowling, pulling the metallic sheets closer to his body. . . .

"No," he mutters, "no, I said, no. Get back. No. Go away. Go away."

The boy, a medi-patch on his forehead, holding on to his mother for warmth, watches his father, listens to the indistinct sentences, his eyes two watery points reflecting the pallid light of stars over this dark world, so quiet, everything so quiet, nothing makes a sound, nothing, nothing loud filling up his ears, no explosion, no tearing of metal, no whoosh of air, no thunderous crash, no screams, nothing, nothing makes a sound, not his mother shivering in her sleep, not his sisters lying in their mound of Martian sand, not the *cohete* snapped in two like a bone, not the smashed radio drained of static, its batteries dead, not his muscles aching from a day of digging, hauling, searching, not even his own heart, beating, beating so quiet, everything so quiet, so still, except the old man, el viejo mumbling, barking at the shadows inside him, tossing beneath the metallic blanket he refuses to share, the old man's squeaky voice of a bat, bouncing weakly on el cohete's broken walls that let in starlight, the old man warm under his silver sheet but still he's mumbling like a child, as the boy watches, silently, the old man mumbling, mumbling. . . .

"Go away. No. No."

With a sullen look, he undid the doll from its tangled prison of cables. In the campfire light its red hair made ragged shadows along its face, which smiled up at him. He sucked on his foul-smelling cigarette, filling his lungs with its filth. Stared at the doll. It escaped the crash without injury, without a scorch mark or stain of blood. There had been no need to sift through the wreckage for it, no need to pull its burned meat in strips from the cohete's hold. No need to salvage its dress for fire fuel, to take it, trying not to gag, piece by piece, limb by limb, in crisp pulpy heaps to the pit, no need to toss it in, a mass of rags and bone and curdled organs like jellyfish, and cover it up with sand. The doll had simply lain there in its nest of wires, waiting for him to find it, smiling and happy.

The old man took the doll to the fire, stood impassively, gazed at the flames. Threw it in. In a minute it had melted into brown slag and plastic smoke, noiselessly. Again he noticed the storm howl, unending, rising. It irritated him. The wind was getting stronger, louder. The sand leaping up, catching the wind, slowly choking the fire. His body tensed, like a rusty spring. The storm. Gritted his teeth. Eyes narrowed to black slits at the storm he couldn't see, only feel, hear, taste, its sand on his lips. The rage coursed through his veins, like the booze, the cigarette's filth, warm, electric. Suddenly he coughed, spit out the particles of sand, the rage flaring. He turned to his wife, still sitting uselessly at her makeshift kitchen, huddled near the fire.

The tamales simmering in the pot, suspended over the fire, rocked lightly by the wind. Tucked in their corn husk beds, the tamales submerged in the hot water, in layers, added slowly, first one layer, then another on top, then another, then another. Not long. Not too long. The boy would wait, swinging his legs in his seat. Not long. Long enough for the dough to harden, congeal, for the *pasas* and sugar to heat up. For when the dough no longer sticks to the husk. The water at a simmer, only a simmer. Not too much flame. Just enough. Just a little. When the dough no longer sticks, they're ready. Almost ready, m'ijito. The tamales, almost ready.

"I told you to stop that," growled the old man. Flung his cigarette into the fire. Kicked up more dust into the wind. Lumbered toward her.

~ ~ ~

He wanders the town, a stooping old man in a cream-colored hat like any other. Booze, bad cigarettes on his breath. The bars, rich people's houses where he mows yards for beer money, six a.m. Sunday mass, his daughters' homes. He comes every week, sits in the kitchen, mumbling for hours in a squeaky, irritating voice, about things his grandchildren casually ignore. They nod, fidget, waiting for their mother to quietly gesture, freeing them from this prattling viejito to the release of the television. Even their mother fidgets, finally tells him she has an errand to run, slips money in his hand at the door, payment for an afternoon's boredom. He leaves, his bent-over lope. Sometimes he walks along the very middle of the road. He starts asking his grandchildren for money, in a mumble they can barely make out now. Only Amparo understands. Amparo just knows he has another woman, though he is well past seventy. "Por ahí tiene una vieja," she tells her grandson. "Don't give him money. No le des. He'll just spend it on his vieja cantinera." "Mentiras," he mutters, scowling weakly in his armchair. Their house grows quiet. The daughters are married, scattered. He keeps the lawn tidy. Grandchildren and great-grandchildren. The son, the youngest, lives with them, slowly drinking himself to death, bearing the brunt of Cruz's worst deprecations, half-uttered now through toothless gums. Every year the son sinks deeper and deeper into himself, away from his father, away from everything, down the numbing spiral. More and more, Cruz has trouble remembering things, except for a past he cannot articulate, in which his descendants take no interest.

"Son of a bitch!" the old man yells as he slips. He falls from the cohete's metal rib that snaps beneath his weight. He falls on his elbows, his face plunging into the orange sand, as the boy, watching at a distance, near his mother, sees his father fall from atop the cohete and suddenly, sin querer, the boy laughs. . . .

The old man curses, shakes off the powdery dust, thinking, thinking he needs to climb up there, he needs to see, the radio, before it died, the radio warned of the storm, stuck in the Martian desert on a goddamn coyote's cohete chingado and the satlink useless and the radio before it died warned of the sandstorm and the land is too flat, and the old man is thinking, thinking that he has to get up there to see, to el cohete's tip, to see where the storm is, from up there you can see for miles, he's thinking, thinking he has to get up there but he can't, the metal's too thin, he's thinking, sweating, wiping his brow in the yellow heat, thinking how to get up there, thinking about the *cohete*'s nose, and then the boy's laugh rings in his ears as the wind picks up and the reddish sun stands right at the tip of the cohete. . . .

"Ven pa cá," the old man commands. "Ven pa cá, I said."

~ ~ ~

"I told you I don't want any!" he yelled at her. "Stupid puta*!* What good are your tamales now? We're dead, I said! We're dead! We're already dead!"

The night wind shrieked louder all around him as he pulled her by the wrist away from her trunk, as he pushed her down to the earth, as he proceeded to kick and tear and break apart her dishes, turn over the crate, spill the dough and husks and rags onto the ground. Watching, her face never changed expression.

"We're dead, mujer. We're all dead! Fuck your tamales de mierda! What good are they now? What good are they now?"

He grabbed the metal pot and screeched, his hands burnt. The pain stopped his thinking, the rage swelled, he lashed out, reasonless, kicked at the large metal pot with his boot, as the wind gusted, as la vieja lay where she'd been thrown in the dust, as the howl filled his ears.

The pot spilled onto the fire as the old man lost his balance, the water met the flames with a loud hiss, throwing up clumps of half-burned fuel, debris and clothing that the wind flung upwards—into his face. The fire crackled, blazed as it devoured the husks, the dough, discharging a sickly-sweet smell of corn, sugar, pasas giving up their juice, smoldering.

The old man screamed, his hands pressed to his face, seeming to dance with the flames all about his legs. He screamed as he fell away from the fire, his hat flying, rolling, snatched away by the ravenous wind, the old man kicking and twisting, his scream mingling with the wind, swinging one lanky arm wildly all about him, feeling his fist strike soft flesh, struggling like an animal as he felt his burning trousers doused with sand, felt the arms of his wife trying to pull his hands away. He pushed himself from her, still swinging his fist, and turned, buried his forehead in the cool sandy earth, screaming, screaming, feeling his mouth fill up with dust as the spitting sparks in his eyes died away to blackness.

They cross the river, the whole family, the shallow part at midnight, because Cruz is tired of going back and forth. The coyotes are kind, they offer their own secluded house near the river on the other side, to hide them, give them a place to sleep. The coyotes are kind, an old man and his son, but they are still coyotes and they demand a stiff price. Strong and healthy at thirty-five, Cruz works in a steel factory in Pennsylvania, but quits when the smoke starts to poison his lungs, as it did his brother's. He does not give up his tarry, unfiltered cigarettes, though. They pick vegetables, migrate with the seasons:

Louisiana, Ohio, Michigan, California and back to Texas. The whole family works, living in company shacks. They fight horribly, but never lay a hand on the children. Cruz only yells and terrifies them into submission, taking out his belt for those who insist on disobedience, the ones who sneak out to meet boys in the town behind his back. Once a week he takes them for a burger and a movie. That should be enough for them. The family saves up to buy a house; finally, they settle. Al fin Amparo gives him eight children, the last the only son.

❧ ❧ ❧

The boy doesn't want to, he tells his father, he doesn't want to, he's saying, "I can't do it, please don't make me do it," he hangs his bandaged head before the old man in front of the *cohete*, the sun bearing down on his scrawny frame, but the old man won't stop pushing him, telling him to climb up there, he's the only one, he has to climb up there and tell him where the storm is, "It's nothing," he says, "it's nothing, el cohete's ribs will hold you, so get up there, it's nothing," and the boy tries to look up at his father but the sun burns his eyes, its flash filling up his vision and he sees only a hard silhouette with a hat looming over him, the blinding sun over its shoulder, he can't see, but he says please in his tiny voice and the old man pushes him, saying, "No es nada, no es nada, you'll go up and come down, what's the matter, you act like a girl, you act like your dead sisters, get up there, it's nothing, I said, get up there and show me where the storm is, this land is too flat."

The boy, hesitating, slowly climbs up the rib of the cohete, unsteady, the hot sun making little circles in his vision, looking with wide eyes back at his mother, round and sad by a heap of clothes, as the old man tells him, "See, it's nothing, I told you, it's nothing, go higher, I said, it's nothing."

The wind's howl, deafening now. Swirls of dust, spinning all around, the fire long dead. The stars, snuffed out. Black, strangulating sand. The old man, his eyes tenderly bandaged, and the old woman, supporting him, the two before a tiny heap of earth, disintegrating in the gale. Just visible in the shifting, baying murk, a white cross made of *cohete* pipes.

On their wedding night the sheet is stained with a faint red splotch. Afterwards he commands her to take the linen outside and wash it, in the darkness. With every motion of her hands on the cloth she feels the painful wet rip inside her, moving. She washes the spot clean away and returns to him.

The boy balances on the very nose of the cohete, his father and mother now small enough to hold in his hands, Mars grown massive and flat in all directions, he a tick on the bump of a huge orange ball, the sun feeling good on his face now, the wind, the thin air, he giggles, giddy, looks about for the storm like his father tells him, "Look around," he says, "tell me where the storm is," he stretches, strains out to see more of the horizon, looking for the storm, his father was right, no era nada, easy, he's so light, he cranes his neck in all directions, *no es* nada, the wind pleasantly in his hair, he hears. . . .

He hears his mother yelling something, his father, calling out to him, he hears the creak, feels the swaying of the cohete, something somewhere snapping. . . .

And the boy slips, he falls, falling, falling more slowly in the Martian gravity, reaching out frantically, convulsing, spinning, tumbling like an injured bird, down, down, the earth rushing up in a final flash of the sun. . . .

Before the muffled, sickening snap. . . .

La vieja hardly moves, takes a few steps, stops, stares at the cloud of orange dust by el cohete, her husband shuffling toward it, throwing up more dust behind him, staring vacantly she feels something go, and without a word, a sound, without anything at all, she collapses on her knees in the sand.

Cruz sees her at a village dance, a peasant girl. He is nearly thirty, the son of a bandleader. A hard man who breaks horses. An Appaloosa is his favorite. She is not yet fifteen, a thin girl with black hair like any other, with a name that pleases him. He will take her. Maybe someday he can bring her with him, al otro lado. Her name is Amparo. Un nieto, nacido allá, would confuse her name with "lámpara"—lamp—and think of her as light. Only later would he know amparo does not mean light. Amparo means "shelter." Amparo.

"It was nothing, I told him, just go up and come down, I said, that's all, that's all, just go up and come down," says the old man, talking as he's done for the last hour, mumbling, shouting, saying the same things again and again, saying, "It's not my fault, you hear, it's not my fault," as he pats down the mound with his shovel and starts to fashion his crude cross and bends his head, listening for the wind, but talking, talking, grumbling all the time. . . .

The old woman sits by the grave, staring at the fresh, dry earth, unmoving, thinking, thinking of something, thinking of getting up, of finding her pots and bowls, and the other things she'll need. . . .

She's thinking, thinking of tamales . . . tamales de azúcar, the boy's favorite . . . tamales de azúcar. . . .

⁂

The sandstorm, a blanket of bees, angry, stinging, buzzing, loud. Everything, everything penetrated by the sound, bones, shaking, pierced. Wind. El cohete, coming apart like straw. Metal, memory, flesh, shredding, dissipating, absorbed. Hot Martian sand, lungfuls, burning. Parched throats in the lost hollow of a broken, crumbling cohete. Tears.

El viejo in her arms, head on her bosom: statues, sand-swallowed, cooling, softening, whittling, blanched. El viejo, tight in her embrace, la vieja, cuidándolo. In her body's fragile shelter.

1985

Ruben Quesada

I stand on our lawn
A girl passes like a vanishing shadow
I watch her wait at the corner crosswalk
As birds dart into trees my eyes blur
A car begins to slip across the horizon
Her body flails toward the curb
My mother appears in the crowd
We stand tightly tucked
It's Mary in a dress the color of asphalt
She is the color of skim milk
Months later
Mary's mother
is found in the garage
With the car running
Before we attend her funeral
the radio announces
Rock Hudson is dead
There was no funeral
only a body the color of ash

1987

Ruben Quesada

On broadcast television
I watch R Budd Dwyer
He gives his life away
He is about to speak
live and direct
before a group of reporters
but they are tired
of this story
Why is this news?
This will hurt someone
says a voice
as thick as skin
off-screen
Cameras scream
He holds a revolver
the size of his head
His hand shakes
like a copperhead colt
Until the Holy Spirit
rattles out of his head

A Curious Encounter

mónica teresa ortiz

On January 12, 1993, Chico worked as a farm hand just outside Abernathy, Texas, home to the Antelopes and St. Isidore Catholic Church, upon whose grounds is erected a thirty-foot Crucifix in a box. Most travelers drive through Abernathy on the way to Lubbock or perhaps Abilene or Dallas, and just ride Interstate-27 without stopping. Abilene isn't much to look at but Chico decided to stop anyway back in 1958 and stayed after he found a job as a cowboy on a nearby ranch. He and his wife Fey arrived in Texas from Chihuahua City, Jimenez, Mexico. Neither Chico nor Fey spoke much English, though both understood it. Chico often said: No necesito inglés porque no me pagan para hablar otro idioma—me pagan para cuidar las vacas.

He was fifty-six years old—still ten years away from retiring. He woke up just one minute after four a.m., pulled his slippers out from under his bed, slid his feet inside them and strode directly to the kitchen—without waking Fey, he let her sleep until six a.m. on Sundays. He brewed his morning coffee and heated up a bowl of plain oatmeal. Chico and Fey lived alone in a three-bedroom farmhouse located on the ranch's property, about two miles away from the main house. They had a thirty-four-year-old daughter named Esperanza who taught math at Monterrey High School in Lubbock, and though they welcomed her, her husband and their granddaughter Sofia's visits, Chico and Fey generally preferred solitude.

Fey pushed the covers off herself just before the crack of seven a.m. and dressed hurriedly in the dark. The Spanish mass at St. Isidore began promptly at 8:30 and she wanted to get there before the hall got full. Still half-asleep, Fey scrambled eggs in the black cast iron frying pan, warmed corn tortillas on the burner and put a fresh pot of beans to soak—she intended to make frijoles charros for dinner. Chico exited the bathroom, his thick white hair glistening and slicked back, his snap-button shirt pressed and perfect. He had even shaved his jaw clean from three-day-old stubble.

¿Vas para la iglesia?

No creo.

¿Por qué no?

Porque no quiero.

Bueno. Te queda el cargo de conciencia.

Fey picked up her purse and shut the front door with a quiet click. Chico, in turn, scooped up the Lubbock Avalanche Journal from the kitchen table and retired to his recliner. He read the newspaper front to back until he heard the crunch of the Ford's tires rolling over the gravel two hours later. Fey unlocked the front door and stared down at Chico. His feet still propped up on the ottoman, he did not look up from the Lifestyle's sections.

Él pregunto por ti.

¿Quién?

Padre Francisco.

¿Y qué dijiste?

Pues nada.

Entonces para qué pregunta.

She said nothing and went to the kitchen. Pots and pans banged—then came static crackling from the radio and finally, the voice of Ana Gabriel drifted through the house. Chico set the paper down and grabbed his wool jacket from the hook near the door. He knocked his boots together to get rid of a little mud on the heel, then shoved his feet inside. His toes, calloused and rough like a cow's hide, hid a painful secret. He never told Fey that he had bunions. Later in life (a span of five years), he would be forced to retire his cowboy boots, wear strictly slippers or comfortable running shoes and shuffle from place to place rather than taking his usual long strides.

Voy a ver las vacas.

Lo que tú quieras.

Fey added pieces of bacon to the beans while peering at Chico. She wondered how long he would be able to walk with those terrible bunions. The front door shut and Fey turned the music up louder. She really liked Ana Gabriel.

After saddling his horse, a three-year-old Pinto named Octavio, Chico took his morning rounds along the southern part of the three-mile pasture, always checking the cattle that chewed the grass.

He closed the gate to the Hereford pasture. Near the northern side of the farm (separated by two miles of fence post) grazed the cattle. On his afternoon round, he made his way around the more docile Hereford cattle. Also called Whitefaces, he started his count of the big red cows with big white faces. As the morning fell into the afternoon, Chico recalled how much he enjoyed the nippy air of the Panhandle. The temperature probably dipped just into the mid-forties, but he did not mind. He understood part of the beauty of the farm was living like an old cowboy, taking whatever nature gave him, and not minding.

An old Blue Heeler named Clint roamed among the Hereford, to keep away coyotes or bobcats. Chico rode Octavio slowly among the herd, looking around for Clint. He whistled for the Blue Heeler, and in a few seconds, Clint barked, then limped up to Chico, his fur ruffled and matted with blood. Chico could see a small wound on Clint's back leg, one that looked like a bite, like another animal had ripped through Clint's sturdy leg. Chico made his way to the back of the herd, the strays nearest the barbed wire fence that marked the end of the farm. He cocked the rifle he carried. He used the rifle only to shoot and scare off would-be predators, but generally, he tried to avoid shooting it among the herd. A rifle shot caused them to stampede, and Chico didn't want to spend the afternoon calming and gathering. As he gazed out of the distance, he discerned a dead cow, one fallen at the edge of the barbed wire fence. Chico rode toward the body and dismounted, pushing the flank with the tip of his boot. He could just make out two tiny puncture wounds near its belly. Chico could not see any traces of blood. He was not sure what had killed the Whiteface. Puzzled, Chico glanced out across the plains, searching the galaxy of prairie grass. He scanned the fence for any opening that would have allowed a coyote or bobcat through to the herd. Clint barked and Chico hurried to the growling dog.

About twenty feet away from where he and Clint stood, a shadow leaped over the fence, then scurried into the brush, to an area where the grass was as high as Chico's waist. Weeds parted as the animal skipped out and then he could see it no longer. Chico aimed his rifle but could not focus. It resembled the shape of a man or some strange dog. He lowered his gun. Clint did not try to chase the thing and the cattle mewled loudly, frightened by the movement and noise. Chico watched the shadow make its way into the distance and thought he caught the scent of sulfur.

Just after nine p.m. that Sunday night, Chico opened the front door and found Fey kneading dough to make flour tortillas. Her large knuckles crushed the white dough into the table, and there beside her were rows of perfect fist-sized balls. Hair pulled up and back in a tight bun, her sleeves rolled up to her elbows, she kept glancing at the television screen. The popular show "The X-Files" was on. Chico did not get why a God-fearing woman such as his wife would watch anything about the supernatural—but at the moment, the dark event of the day spoiled his mind.

Una vaca está muerta.

¿Qué la mato?

No sé. Yo creo que fue el diablo.

No seas estúpido.

En serio. La criatura se chupó toda la sangre del animal.

¿Qué dices?

Vi algo en el zacate.

¿Qué viste?

Un enano colmilludo. Negro y ojos rojos.

Eso te paso por ateo, malcristiano.

No te burles que lo vi con estos ojos.

Fey stopped what she was doing and looked directly at Chico. They had married in 1957, moved to the United States in 1958 against the protestations of her parents, and on February 2, 1959, Buddy Holly died in a plane crash. She suddenly remembered the newspaper reporting the death of the singer. Originally from Lubbock, Holly left behind a young widow named María Elena. Neither Chico nor Fey mourned Buddy Holly—they did not know his music—but both encountered a deep sympathy for his wife. They had watched several news reports about the plane crash, and during one show, when the camera caught his widowed bride (pregnant at the time) exiting a building, Chico's hazel eyes, for a moment, had gone afraid. He had turned to Fey (pregnant at the time) and remarked: ¿Qué hago yo si te paso algo, quién me va cuidar? She had replied: No seas tonto. But she was secretly pleased.

Fey studied Chico standing in the doorway—picking apart every crack and crag and line in his handsome face; she wanted to dismiss his ridiculous story about a murderous devil sucking the blood of the cattle, but she saw the same fear in his eyes as she did in 1959—a struggle to comprehend an idea that he was incapable of understanding.

She wiped her floured hands on her apron and walked to him, then planted a small kiss on his cheek. No te preocupes. Seguro era el chupacabra.*

---

* Jorge Luis Borges forgot one animal when he wrote *The Book of Imaginary Beings*. It did not exist at the time—or at least had not been reported.

El Chupacabra now runs wild all over the Southwestern United States, mostly on the borders of Texas, New Mexico, Arizona and California. The word "*chupacabra*" translates from Spanish into English as "goat sucker." Such a curious name came from the early history of farmers and ranchers finding dead goats (and other livestock) with small puncture wounds upon their necks and completely exsanguinated. Originating in Puerto Rico during the 1970s after a rash of UFO sightings, the little monster made its way stateside and into the US Mexican folklore. Sometimes El Chupacabra is bipedal, near five feet tall, with a flat bald head, usually grey-colored (similar to the clay-made humanoid aliens on display in the UFO Museum in Roswell, New Mexico), three-fingered clawed hands, a reptilian hide (think smooth and thick-like crocodile skin), an oval head and an elongated jaw. Some witnesses claim that El Chupacabra sports two red (or black) beady eyes, a slit for a mouth and a serious over and underbite. There are reports that El Chupacabra stinks like sulfur and resembles mostly a tiny vampire. According to some reports, El Chupacabra manifests itself as an intelligent being and possesses some rudimentary skill of invisibility. Theories vary as to how El Chupacabra came into the world. Some say it is the result of secret government experiments in genetics; still others maintain that El Chupacabra is an alien from a fifth dimension sent to earth to warn the human race about the progress of technology and the human need to play God. However, some believe El Chupacabra is indisputably unreal, a myth—because vampires are a mathematical impossibility.

Chola Salvation

Estella Gonzalez

I'm just kicking back, drinking my dad's Schlitz, when Frida Kahlo and the Virgen de Guadalupe walk into our restaurant. La Frida is in a man's suit, a big baggy one like the guy from the Talking Heads, but this one's black, not white. All her hair is cut off so she isn't wearing no braids, no ribbons, no nothin'. The only woman thing she has on are those hand earrings. I read in Mrs. Herrera's class that Pablo Picasso gave her those earrings because he thought she was a better painter than her husband.

La Virgen looks like my *tía* Rosa in the picture she sent to Dad. She has blonde hair, lots of white eyeshadow and she's wearing chola clothes. You know, tank top with those skinny little straps, baggy pants and black Hush Puppy shoes. And she has on this lipstick like she just bit a chocolate cake. Her hair is so long, it touches the back of her feet. Her bangs are all sprayed up, like a regular chola, but she wears a little gold crown. A bad-ass *vata loca* sitting at the counter right in front of me.

At first, I don't recognize them but the moment I see Frida's unibrow and La Virgen's crown, I know. I really know for sure the moment Frida gives me a cigarette, even though there's this big ol' sign right at the counter saying, "Thank you for not smoking." I suck on it while La Virgen holds up a lighter.

"*¿Qué ondas, comadre?*" Frida says, smiling. "Whassup?"

One of her teeth is missing and some of the others are all brown. No wonder she never smiles in her paintings. I don't know what to say, so I just take another swig from the beer I have behind the counter.

"Are you a shy girl?" La Virgen says. "Don't you know us, *esa*?"

"Man, sure I know you guys," I shout. I always shout when I'm a little buzzed. "You want some coffee or something?"

"*Un cafecito y un platillo de menudo.*"

"*¿Y tú, Friducha?*"

"How about some *pozole y unas cuantas tortillas de maíz,*" she says.

So, I serve them their menudo, pozole, tortillas and coffee. They tell me they're here to give me some advice: *unos consejos*.

"And believe me, you're going to need the advice, *preciosa*," Frida says. "Because your crazy Mami is going to let you have it with this whole *quinceañera* bullshit real soon."

La Virgen nods and takes another puff.

"We're here to tell you, you better watch out," La Virgen says. "So we have some rules for you to live by. You know, like those Ten Commandments Father Jorge taught you."

"Yeah, but this isn't about God, Jesus or some other Catholic laws," Frida says, ripping up her last tortilla.

"It's about you, homegirl, and about your *pinche* parents and this quinceañera they wanna force down your throat," La Virgen tells me. "You probably don't wanna hear it from me, especially since your mom is always throwing me in your face, saying how much you're hurting me every time you don't listen to her . . . but I want you to hear it from me, not something your mom picked up from your *abuela.*"

I pull up a chair. I'm puffing away, the smoke relaxing me. I don't even feel sick, like those stupid films at school say you're supposed to. It's Sunday and Mom has been at church since 6 am. She usually stays away until about 10, because she sells *buñuelos* and tamales out in front of the church to people getting out of Mass. The restaurant's empty except for the three of us. I go over and lock the door, close the blinds, turn over the "Closed" sign and scooch a chair in between my *comadres.*

Frida leans over to me and takes my hand. La Virgen smiles with her chocolate brown lips.

"*Hermosa* Isabela, your parents say they just want you to be a 'decent' girl," Frida says. "They want you to grow up with all those bourgeoisie ideas. If you have to drink to protect your soul, then do it. Just stop with the cheap beer. You're better off drinking your father's *tequila.*"

Then she pulls out a bottle of El Patrón Silver and three shot glasses. She fills the little glass to the top for me. I take it down in one gulp, and it burns at first, but soon I'm on my second shot, trying to keep up with La Purísima Virgen who's drinking the stuff like it's water.

"How 'bout another?" she asks, handing me another cigarette.

I notice her nails. They're painted blue, covered with little gold stars. It looks like she's holding a galaxy in her hands.

"How about taking up smoking?" Frida says. "*Sí*, I know I'm encouraging vices, but at your age you need all the help you can get. How about drinking? I have no idea when I started but before I knew it, I was challenging Leon Trotsky to tequila shots. *Pobre cabrón*, he was no match for me. Not even in bed."

Then she asks me if I'm still a virgin. When I tell her I am, she shakes her head.

"*Pobrecita* shy girl," La Virgen says. "What? Did your *mamita* tell you to wait 'til your husband popped your cherry?"

Man, she's rough. If she wasn't La Virgen, I'd just think she was another one of those high school skanks. But she's La Virgen. She knows everything and she's just telling it like it is.

"She told me only sluts had sex before they got married," I say. "Those types of women end up pregnant or *putas*."

They both look at each other and laugh again. Frida laughs so hard, she starts rolling around on the floor, kicking her feet. When she gets up, she's wiping tears from her eyes.

"Listen, *preciosa*," La Virgen says. "I don't know if you know this, but your little *pinche* saint of a mother had already started fucking your dad when she was fourteen. But she made the mistake of getting pregnant. Her *mamá, tu abuela*, hadn't bothered to tell her about what girls and boys can do when they're hot for each other."

"If you decide to take up with men, be careful!" Frida says. "Capitalist, communist, they're all the same. If you're not careful, you'll end up like me or, even worse, your mother. I loved a man, a great artist, who just couldn't respect me as a wife. 'Fidelity is for the bourgeoisie,' Diego would say. Well, thanks to the bourgeoisie, I painted the most miserable pieces of art ever. Maybe men aren't so bad . . . now that I think about it. Yes, men are another worthy vice."

Just then, the two of them start arguing over who's fucked the most men.

"Well, *cabrona*, you started like three thousand years before me," Frida gives in.

La Virgen smiles, sucks on her teeth and says, "Yeah, way before Johnny Cortez, I'd already had about 50,000 *papacitos*. Mmmm, maybe more."

"At least I had Trotsky," Frida says.

"And you're proud of that?"

Frida's unibrow scrunches up, and I think for sure she's going to throw her cigarette in La Virgen's face. La Virgen ignores her, makes a toast to men.

"*Ya, cállate*," Frida tries to shut her up. "Can we get back to helping Isabela?"

La Virgen laughs like she's won this one.

"Here are some more tips, homegirl," La Virgen says. "Listen up, *chica*, because we made them up especially for you."

Rule #1: Don't get pregnant. Have as much sex as you like, but don't get pregnant. Not until you really, really wanna. Believe me, I had four hundred sons and a daughter. That was a lot of work. What's worse is that this gang of three, some father, son and ghost, took over my gang while I was spending all my time raising these kids. Now look at this mess!

Rule #2: Go to school. You're gonna have to work the system. Why do you think I appeared like this little *virgencita* with the cutie pie face to Juan Diego and that fat bishop? I'm working this game, *chica*. Now look at me. From Chiapas to Chicago, you see me everywhere: murals, tattoos, books, art. Yeah, Lupe's Ladies are all over. Like that crazy *vato* John Lennon once said about Los Beatles, "We're bigger than Jesus Christ."

Rule #3: You're in charge of your *panocha* and don't be afraid to protect it! Some guy is always gonna try to get into your pants, no matter how much you don't wanna. Even your sweet *papacito*. Yeah, don't think we don't know about him. If you have to kick some ass to teach him some respect, do it.

Rule #4: Spread the word. We need to get the word out to all our homegirls and our homeboys, especially the homeboys. Maybe they'll quit with all this macho shit they keep hearing from their families. I think Chuy and his *papá* may be causing all this.

Rule #5: We're all *indias*. Don't let your mom fool you. No one's a hundred percent. Be proud of the *indígena* inside of you. I know your old lady is down on you for behaving like an Apache, but believe me, we can't all be blonde and blue-eyed. Your mom heard the same lies about the white girls being the only ones worth anything from her own *mami*, a pure blood Tarahumara. Morena, you're beautiful too. Check my little brown self out one of these days, hanging in my gold frame right near the altar. I have the place of honor, not these other little wimpy Marías."

I'm wasted but I get the rules down. Suddenly, Frida puts her arm around me. She points to the paper skeletons I hung in a corner for Día de los Muertos.

"Look at those skeletons dancing. They're waiting for you, you know. Before you know it, you'll be fifty instead of fifteen and you'll wonder where your life went. Don't listen to those crazy sons of bitches you call your parents. You better start fighting them off now before you end up like those baby rats your mother found and drowned.

"Don't you have any friends, *muñeca*? That's strange for a girl your age, you know. At your age, I already had a boyfriend and was hanging out with my *clica*. If you had more vices, you wouldn't care so much."

Frida downs another shot of Patrón. Man, she wasn't even sweating.

"This is the most important thing I wanted to tell you: Ms. Herrera thinks you have a good eye for art. I bet you draw circles around your classmates. What do you think? Maybe art should be your vice. That would really drive your parents crazy, because they wouldn't understand. Smoking, drinking and fucking—those things they understand, because that's what they grew up with, that's what they lived. Art will be your world. You can create your own reality. Then you can escape this capitalistic quinceañera caca they're trying to feed you."

Frida lifts the bowl to her mouth and slurps the rest of her pozole. La Virgen takes another drag from her cigarette, drops it on the floor and stubs it out with her foot.

"Listen, *preciosa*, you'll probably think I'm a miserable pig, but you have to do something before your parents destroy you. Take this advice from me, La Friducha, whom you say you admire so much. Just forget about Father Jorge, all the *tías* and *tíos*, and just go with your gut. Believe me, you don't want the Pelona to get you while you're living some kind of middle-class hell. You'll thank me for it later."

Frida stands up and looks at her watch.

"Wait for me, *cabrona*," La Virgen says as she pulls out her compact mirror and puts on more chocolate brown lipstick.

"Just because you like going around painted like Bozo, doesn't mean I have to wait," Frida says. "We have other *carnalas* we gotta help."

"Hey, I'm not the one going around with a mustache over my lip and eyes."

"*Pinche puta*. You wanna take it outside?"

"*Tranquila*," La Virgen says. "I'm just kidding, homes."

They're leaving. I know if I ask them to stay, they won't. If they meet Mom, they'll kill her.

"We have to go," La Virgen says. "Another *carnal* needs our help. What? You never knew about my bad-ass chola side? Chica, in this crazy world sometimes you don't have a choice."

Before they leave, they both kiss me on the cheek. Frida hugs me real hard. La Virgen leaves me her last cigarette so I can remember her whenever I look at it. I see the brown lipstick mark where she sucked on it.

"*Adiós, muñeca,*" Frida says. "Don't forget the rules."

I cry so hard after they leave because I know I won't see them for a long time. Just after they disappear, Mom shows up holding a white dress.

"*M'ija*, look what I bought you. Isn't it beautiful?" she says.

Mom's been shoving the whole thing in my face since I turned fourteen. She even gets the *tías* to nag me about it. Dad doesn't do it so much but he's starting to get on me about my weight. It never bothered him before, but now it's always, "Why can't you fix yourself up? Get out and do something. Pluck your eyebrows. What man is gonna want you?"

Yeah, I'm too fat and ugly for other guys, but not for him when he starts touching me in the shower or when he feels me up in the car. He never says nothing. He just looks at me the way other guys look at the girls at school. La Virgen's right. I have to protect my *panocha,* even from my own dad.

Then, here comes Mom with her stupid quinceañera dress and all her dumb ideas about a big party with *mariachis* and everything. All that stuff costs, and I know they don't have the money. Even I know our crummy restaurant barely cuts it every month, especially now that there's a Pollo Loco on the corner.

Frida and La Virgen were right. Mom just wants to show off how well she raised me. Please. She can shove it. Just like that stupid white dress. Who told her to buy it anyway?

"Mom, I told you I don't want a quinceañera."

"But don't you want to wear this and look beautiful in front of your friends?"

"I don't have any friends."

"*Ay, no seas tan sangrona*," she says, calling me stubborn and shoving the dress at me.

I throw it back at her and run back to the house. Dad doesn't even look up from his soccer game when me and Mom run right between him and the TV. I run into my room but can't lock the door in time. She just pushes the door real hard and busts in.

"*¡Niña malagradecida!*" she says. "Ungrateful brat! This dress cost me $300! Do you think I'm just going to throw it away?"

She still has the dress with her. As I try to hide in the closet, she grabs me by the shirt and starts slapping me.

Then I slap her back, and that's when she loses it. She takes a step back a little and then punches me in the gut. When I fall doubled over on my bed, she grabs me around the waist and sits me up. That *vieja* is strong for a short woman. It's her Tarahumara Indian blood. She's always bragging about how all her strength comes from her blood.

"*A chingao*, is that cigarette smoke I smell on you?" she grumbles, sniffing like a hound. "Where did you get them? Did you steal them from your father?"

I wait for her to slap me again, but she just picks up the dress and hangs it on the door. I lie down because I feel like barfing.

"You used to be such a good girl, so obedient, and now, *como un pinche apache!*"

She comes right up to me, leans over and tears down my Frida Kahlo poster, "My Birth." It's my favorite poster, and she knows it. But it's always bugged the shit out of her because it's not one of those pretty pictures of a puppy with big sad eyes or a ballerina girl. No, my poster shows a dead mother with a dead baby hanging out of her between her legs. It shows everything, even the mother's vagina covered in black pubic hair. What I really like about it is the painting of the Nuestra Señora de Dolores hanging over the bed. She's the real mother, because like all mothers, she's always in pain and makes everyone around her feel it. Mom calls it disgusting and starts ripping it into little pieces.

"There," she says when she's done. "Maybe you won't hit your own mother next time."

Before she leaves, she turns to the little bust of the Virgen de Guadalupe hanging over my door. I hear her say something stupid, like "*Ayúdame, Virgencita.*"

After she leaves, I lock the door, grab the bust and throw it out the window. That stupid dress. I wasn't about to look like a big white whale for her. Just because her *comadres*' daughters had theirs doesn't mean I have to go through this. She's not fooling me. This is about her. She wants to let everybody know her daughter's like all the other daughters, ready to get fucked. It's not bad enough that I'm fat and that everybody makes fun of me at home and at school, but now Mom wants to embarrass me in front of some crowd at church. Anyway, who's going to be stupid enough to be my escort? Tina's my only friend, and she dropped out of school last year and moved out to Coachella with her mom, so, I hardly see *her*.

Jesus, I haven't been to church for weeks now, so who cares? Dad never goes. He just stays home and watches soccer games. That's why I never take showers on Sundays. 'Cause I know the moment he hears the water running, he'll come right in to feel me up. One time I locked the door, and he got so mad, he almost broke the door down. When Mom got home, he told her some bullshit lie that I shouldn't lock the door because I might slip and fall, and nobody would be able to help me. Of course, Mom believed it. He says it's my fault because I'm fat. He's doing me a favor because no boy is gonna want some fat slob like me. He says it's my fault that Mom gets so mad at me, she won't fuck him. So I have to at least let him touch my tits and pussy. That's the only good thing for him about my being fat. At least I have big tits.

I grab some scissors out of my drawer and I start stabbing the dress. Then, before I know it, I cut it up into little pieces, even the big lace bow on the dress's butt.

I don't care. Just like Mom doesn't care about punching me in the belly or calling me a *pinche apache*. So what if it cost $300? Who asked her to buy it?

When I see all these little pieces of white on the floor, I freak out. They just sit there all shiny and white, staring up at me. I feel like I killed something.

I know it's a sign from the Virgen because the white shreds remind me of all the little stars on her hands. I've gotta get out. I feel real crazy and macho at the same time, like Dad when he gets drunk. This time I'm not gonna chicken out. This time, it's for real, and I'm not coming back. So I dig out some money from under my bed, pack up my duffel bag and jam to downtown LA. When I get to the Greyhound, I hide out in the bathroom until 2 in the morning and catch the first bus to El Paso.

I wake up the next day to a stinkin' pile of sweat. God does that fat lady smell. Her hair is all stringy and half her ass is over on my side of the seat. Yeah, she's fat like me. Maybe I stink too. That really bums me out. Maybe it's me that's smelling up this whole bus. I look over the seat in front of me. Naaah. Other people look like they stink too. The next stop, I'm gonna wash my pits just to make sure. I could use some of that fancy soap I stole from Mom. She always got pissed when I tried to use it. I loved the way it smelled, like that perfume in J.C. Penney's. It smelled even nicer than Dial.

I look at the fat lady's watch. It's barely 10 a.m. The guy at the bus station said we wouldn't get to El Paso until 8. Shit.

When the bus stops, at Blythe this time, I go wash my pits, my feet and my neck. This lady walks in. She's crying, looks like she's been punched in her eye. I pack my stuff up real fast.

"*M'ija*," she says to me, "you have some tissue?"

"Nah," I say. "There's some toilet paper here, though."

"Could you get me some?"

I get her some.

She's wiping her face, and her eye looks Chinese because it's all slanted and almost closed.

"Don't ever get married, sweetie," she says, like she's laughing.

I just try to walk real slow to the door.

"Don't ever marry a guy who drinks," she says. Now she's crying real hard.

"My dad drinks," I say, then I wish I'd kept my mouth shut.

"Yeah?" She turns to me. "So did mine."

I just get real scared when she tells me that. She sounds just like Mom. I feel like getting on that bus and driving it to El Paso myself. When I get back on, I sit way in the back, right next to the toilet, so I don't have to hear that lady cry. Jesus, when the hell are we getting out of here? Outside, it's just red rocks and hills, sometimes little bushes. There's barbed wire all over the place, as if anybody would want to climb over that. It's so fuckin' hot on the bus, but I won't take off my sweatshirt. I just have my muscle shirt on, no bra. I'm not trying to be sexy. I just forgot to take any bras with me. Anyway, I see this slimy guy look at me weird. . . . I don't need anybody hassling me right now. Of course, when the bus gets going and I get up, some asshole has to say something.

"Hey, fat ass, can you get your stomach out of my face?" some old woman says.

"Fuck off," I say. "I'm just trying to get my duffel bag."

The stupid lady punches me in the gut. I fall over on the guy who gave me that weird look. He cops a feel when I try to get up. I almost pop him one, when the bus driver stops the bus.

"Hey, you! Don't start any trouble or I'll leave you right here."

I roll my eyes real hard, grab my duffel bag and head back to my seat. *What else can I do?* The last thing I need is for him to leave me here in the middle of nowhere or maybe call the cops. After digging around my bag, I find the picture of Tía Rosa sitting on her boyfriend's lap. She's holding a cigarette. Looks like he's squeezing her. A big margarita glass sits on the table next to them. She's laughing. Her lips are red-red, like a Crayola crayon, and her hair is short and gold, like Blondie's. On the back of the picture she wrote: "*Con mucho cariño y amor para mi sobrina Isabela, de parte de tu Tía Rosa. Aquí estoy con mi novio Pablo en el restaurante Ajúúa! Visítame cuando quieras. Mi número de teléfono es 13-16-57. Mi dirección es Avenida 16 de Septiembre 3555, Juárez. Los espero.*"

That's her address: Avenida 16 de Septiembre in Juárez. I wonder if she wanted to invite all of us, or just me. I guess she thought I'd be coming with Mom and Dad. I don't think she really liked Mom, though. One time, at a party, Tía was dancing to a *cumbia*, "*Tiburón, Tiburón*," with Uncle Beto. She looked like that statue of Our Lady of Fatima with her small angel lips, dark eyes and pale skin. She wore her short blue dress. Mom was in the kitchen serving the *carne asada* Dad had just cooked up outside.

"*Vieja sinvergüenza*," she said when I walked in with all the paper plates. "Your aunt just likes shaking her butt in front of everybody."

"She's a good dancer."

"She should be helping me in the kitchen."

"Where's Tía Amelia?"

"She's helping your father cook the steaks."

A little while later, I saw Uncle Beto taking Mom by the hand and trying to make her dance. Mom laughed, shook her head. Dad tried to take out Tía Rosa, but she said no and walked outside to the patio. Instead of going back to the party, he came after me, but I split onto the patio with Tía Rosa. She was sitting there smoking and singing, "*Zandunga*."

"*¿Qué pasa, muñeca?*" she said.

I could smell her Coco Chanel perfume mixing with the smoke. "Nothing."

"Want a cigarette?"

"Yeah!"

I took a little puff. I still believed my dumb health teacher when she said smoking made you sick. I didn't want to embarrass myself in front of Tía, so I just made sure not to breathe in too deeply. We just smoked and listened to all my other aunts, uncles and cousins whooping it up in the house. I just wanted to sit there and smoke forever. Tía just kept singing until Uncle Beto came out looking for her.

"I'll be there in a minute," she said, lighting up another cigarette. "What a pain in the ass."

"Can I have another one?"

"Already? Why are you smoking so much? You're only thirteen."

"I don't know. I just hate being here."

"Me too."

Tía started singing another Mexican song. Beto came out again, and this time she got up. After a while, Mom came out looking for me and told me to "play" with my cousins. Jesus, I was thirteen. It's not like I was playing with *pinche* Barbies. I went back into the house and the first thing I saw was Dad dancing with my baby cousin Evelina. At first, I couldn't believe it was him. Everybody was dancing real fast and jerky to a *cumbia*, but he was dancing slowly so he wouldn't step on Evelina's little shoes. I remember I wanted to cry so bad, I ran into the kitchen, grabbed a beer out of the fridge and just sat outside waiting for everybody to leave.

Before Tía left, she gave me another cigarette and asked me to go visit her. That was before she and Uncle Beto divorced. After the divorce, Mom never let me go and visit her. Dad told me the same bullshit that Tía Rosa was a *vieja sinvergüenza*. Uncle Beto married some other woman he'd met at a cabaret and didn't visit us anymore.

No big loss. I never liked the fucker anyway.

I can see from the bus window that outside it's getting brighter and hotter. I break out my notebook and start drawing an old chola with big feathered hair. First, I draw her skinny, then I draw her fat like me, with big boobs coming out the sides of her muscle shirt. When I look up, everything looks melted. I close my eyes and try to forget about the stink and the crying. I pretend like I'm dead and I finally go to sleep.

After getting to El Paso and crossing the bridge to Juárez, I take a bus I think goes by Tía's house. I get off on September 16th Street, right where the bus driver tells me. All I smell is rotten mangoes and car fumes. It's so hot out here, and my pits are already dripping. God, I forgot how poor everybody is here, especially the *indios* and the little kids. Mom was always hassling me about throwing me out with the *indios*. There ain't that many in East LA. Now I know why she thought it was a big deal. Jesus, they're really poor. I see a mother and kids sitting on the sidewalk. She's dividing up what the kids have brought in begging.

I once knew a guy named Indio. All the kids used to call him that. I think his real name was Arturo. He used to hang out with all the other winos on the corner of our block.

"*Pinche indio,*" Dad used to say. "All they ever do is beg and drink. They don't know the meaning of work."

I always wanted to ask Dad why he said that. Mom was half Tarahumara and I know Grandma, Dad's mom, was pure *india*. One time when I braided my hair just like Laura Ingalls on "Little House on the Prairie," he called me a *pinche india fea*. He was pissed. I look at my braids now. They're like the baskets I see for sale on the sidewalk.

God this place is dirty. I don't want to look at the little Indian girl with her little brown girl face selling chiclets in her yellow dress so bright she looks like a sun. She walks back to her mom, who's now sitting on some steps. The woman starts yelling at her.

The little girl runs back to me. Poor kid. Her mom probably beats the shit out of her if she doesn't sell enough of those stupid little gums.

"*Niña, dame dos paquetitos.*"

I give her a quarter, even though I know I better save my money. I hope I don't have to stay at some motel or something. What should I tell Tía? Should I tell her about Mom and the dress? What if she sends me back to LA? I hope she doesn't make me go back. What if she calls the police? Then I'm booking it, because there's no way I'm staying in a Mexican jail! Well, if I can't stay here, I'm going to Mexico City and visiting Frida's house. Maybe I can hide out there for a little while. At least I can see that before I have to go back. Jesus, I don't think I can hold out until I'm eighteen.

Maybe if I told Tía about Mom punching me? But then I'd have to tell her why. Shit. Maybe she'll understand because she hates Mom too. I think she does. I wonder if she knows Mom thinks she's a slut. I don't know if I can tell her about the dress. Jesus, it stinks here. Or maybe it's me. I haven't showered in days. Maybe I should tell her about Dad. I can't believe I'm here. I hope I don't have to go back. Mom'll kill me for sure.

"*¡Oye, mamacita!*" a male voice slurs.

I keep walking real fast.

"*¡Tú! ¡Gordita!*"

I see some guy with a cowboy hat waving at me. Jesus fuck. Now he's walking alongside me.

"*Bonita, ¿estás sola? ¿Quieres un novio?*"

He looks at me the way Dad does when he feels me up. Cowboy guy has a skinny Pedro Infante mustache and he's wearing this thick belt with a huge belt buckle like Dad wears. Shit, my shirt's all sweaty and I know I stink that fat stink. But fuck this, not this time. I'll pop him with my duffel bag if he gets any closer. Cowboy guy's voice sounds far away but he's still walking right behind me, making kissing noises. God, I don't wanna faint out here. I spot a church and walk in real fast.

It's nice and cool but it's so fucking dark. I can't see anything except the altar. I book it right up the middle, sit right up in front with some old ladies and bow my head like I'm praying. I just whisper, whisper, whisper, look around. I don't see him. Then this old lady next to me starts poking me with her elbow.

"I know you're not praying, *esa*," she says. I look at her hands and see those little stars on the nails.

"Virgencita," I sigh. "You scared me. I thought you were one of these *viejas*."

"Hey, some of these *veteranas* are my homegirls," she says.

She's wearing a black rebozo but I can see the little points of her crown sticking up on her head, through the black.

"Virgen," I say, "you have to help me."

She takes me to the side of the church where all the short candles are in front of a saint's statue.

"*¿Qué pasa?*" she says.

"It's this cowboy guy," I say. "He's after me." I start to cry. I don't know why. I hardly ever cry.

"Is he after your *panocha*?"

"Yeah," I say. "He was making kissing noises and calling me 'Mamacita.'"

"Let's go."

When we push the door open, I see him right there, across the street from the church.

"He's right there," I tell the Virgen, "with the cowboy hat."

She starts crossing the street and does one of those shrill whistles, with her fingers in her mouth. It's so loud I can hear her even when a big bus passes right in front of me. Cowboy Dude smiles his little mustache smile and starts walking over to us. La Virgen looks him up and down, like some guy she's about to dance with. La Virgen whips off her *rebozo* and hands it to me. Something shiny sticks out of her pants. It looks like a gun. When she pulls it out, it looks just like that gun in the Dirty Harry movies. Everybody clears out, even the little *indio* kids. Cowboy dude just stops still, drops his little smile. La Virgen starts waving her *cuete* around in front of Cowboy Dude's face, then she puts it right up to his mouth.

"*Bésalo*," she says, telling him to kiss it.

Cowboy Dude just opens his mouth like he's gonna say something.

"*Bésalo, cabrón*," La Virgen says and cocks the gun.

Her tiny finger doesn't look strong enough to squeeze the trigger, but I know she can pop that *cuete* faster than any cowboy. Cowboy Dude puckers up and kisses the gun. A little kiss.

"*Como besas a tus mamacitas*," La Virgen says, meaning, "Like you're in love."

He kisses it again. This time though, he frenches the barrel.

La Virgen smiles, puts her *cuete* back in her pants. Cowboy Dude's legs keep shaking even as we start to walk away. Suddenly, he tries to jump her but only falls down screaming. He's grabbing his crotch and rolling around on the sidewalk. La Virgen looks back at Cowboy Dude, spits right on his face and gives him a good kick in the ribs. All of a sudden, there's a crowd of *indias* around us with their little kids. Some of them are laughing and making the sign of the cross on their heads and chests. Down the block, there are a couple of Mexican cops staring.

La Virgen takes back her *rebozo*, now green and covered with gold stars. "Keep this," she says, handing me the huge gun.

I stick it in my duffle bag as she grabs my arm and pushes me across the street, straight into a purple taxicab.

"Templo Chola Tattoo," La Virgen tells the cab driver. "You're gonna need it," she says, lighting up a cigarette for me.

"Here, drink some of this," she orders, handing me a bottle of Hornitos tequila.

I take a little sip and almost throw up.

I can see the cab driver staring at La Virgen every time we stop. Hasn't he ever seen a chola before? When we get to the tattoo place, Frida's waiting for us at the front door. This time she's dressed in a long skirt and her hair's braided up and wrapped around her head.

"*Hola, muñeca,*" she says hugging me.

I almost fall, I feel so dizzy. "How come we're here?"

"Because your *tía* works here," Frida says.

Inside, I see the blonde woman in my picture working on this big, fat guy's back. She's wearing glasses, and he's wearing thick black shades so tight a little bit of fat hangs over them. I see some women sitting down next to the white, white walls. All around, cartoon pictures hang. My head feels like it's buzzing. It's so bright inside, I want to shut my eyes.

"*Hola, amores,*" Tía Rosa says, not looking up from the fat guy's back. "*Ahoritita les ayudo.*"

All I can hear is the needles buzzing. Two other guys are helping my aunt. I think one of them is her boyfriend Pablo, because he has his long black hair in a ponytail and doesn't look old like Uncle Beto or Dad.

"Frida?" Tía Rosa says. "Lupe? Who do you bring me?"

Tía Rosa knows my *comadres*? I guess she would know them.

"We bring you Isabela," Frida says. "She needs a tattoo, maybe two, to save her."

"Save her from what?" Tía Rosa says.

"From her mother and your brother Rodolfo," Frida says, pulling out a big black book from behind Pablo.

Tía Rosa finally looks like she recognizes me. She grabs my arm and takes us into a back room. On the walls she has pictures of La Virgen and little candles everywhere. On one side is a poster of Frida with a skull on her forehead. I can tell Tía smells the tequila on my breath as she gets in my face, looking closer. She lifts her hand and caresses my cheek.

"Did he touch you?" she asks.

I nod and start to cry like a baby. Then I unload, telling her everything about Mom, the dress and Dad. She gives me some water mixed with sugar.

"You gave her too much tequila," Tía says.

"It was Lupe," says Frida.

"She'll need it, if you're gonna give her a tattoo," La Virgen says.

"We'll do that later," Tía says.

I want to get a tattoo so bad, but I pass out before I can look through the book Frida hands me.

"Why did ya come over to this hellhole?" Mousy says.

We're watching the hookers walk up and down the street in front of the nightclubs trying to find johns. I see the little Indian girls begging the American tourists for money, trying to put on their sad faces, making their little lips puffier and sadder. I can smell old meat and blood from the butcher shop next door.

"I don't know," I say. "Tía lets me smoke as much as I want to. Anyway, she says she'll teach me how to be a tattoo artist."

"You could have learned that back in East Los," she says, passing me her roach.

"No thanks," I say. I tried it once and it made me feel like shit. I think it was laced with Angel Dust or acid or some homemade shit. I'm not chancing it anymore. I'm sticking to cigs and booze, for now.

"At least my old man can't feel me up in the shower anymore."

"Your old man did that? *¡Pinche asqueroso!*"

We can hear Mousy's grandfather playing his accordion in La Rondalla club. His name is Don Ramón and he still plays even though he's pushing eighty. It's sad seeing that old man holding that heavy old accordion and pushing its buttons. Don Ramón is accompanied by two friends, so old they look like they're gonna bite the dust real soon. He has to support Mousy and her mom while her dad's out in California. Supposedly he'll send money back to them. For now, Mousy works at the laundry, washing and ironing clothes. Shit, I'd rather go to school than burn my hands washing clothes in Clorox.

"What time is it?" I ask Mousy.

"It's almost time for the *brujas* to come out."

"I better get back to the house, or Tía's gonna yell at me again for not getting to school on time."

"You're lucky. I have to get my ass out to the laundry by 5."

"See you tomorrow, homegirl."

When I walk into the house, my cousins are wearing out the Atari I got real cheap last week at a secondhand store in El Paso. Noel keeps bugging me for a Walkman, but I can't get one for cheap like the other stuff. Evelina always wants a *saladito* from the corner store. I walk to the kitchen and warm up a tortilla. There's a scorpion on the wall, so I break out the heavy huarache Tía uses to kill them. She won't use Raid because it stinks. Yeah, this whole place is worse than my place in LA, but at least Tía doesn't treat me like some punching bag or her personal *puta*. I even take showers on Sundays now.

As soon as I walk into the kitchen, I see Pablo looking through some of my drawings I left on the table. I feel my stomach getting all tight and I start sweating. Why do guys think they can do whatever they want? Why can't they keep their fuckin' hands to themselves? So I grab the *cuete* out of the duffel bag. Shit, I forgot how heavy it was. That's okay. I can use two hands like that Angie chick does on *Police Woman*.

"Freeze, motherfucker!" I say, real tough, pointing the big ol' gun at his head.

Poor Pablo. I think he's gonna shit right there. He puts the drawings down real slow.

"*Cálmala*," he says. "I was just looking at your drawings, *esa*. Your *tía* asked me to do a tattoo for you, so I thought I could use one of these."

I don't know if I'm just surprised or what. Before I can think, I drop the stupid gun, and I'm lucky it doesn't go off, because the police down here don't fuck around.

Pablo's cool, he doesn't freak out about the whole thing, but I know my *tía*'s gonna trip. Pablo lets me keep my gun and promises not to go through my stuff again without my permission.

"Keep it in Templo's backroom," he says. "That way the kids won't get to it."

Shit, I forgot about my cousins.

I follow him out to the tattoo parlor and stuff the Virgen's gift in the drawer of the little table where Tía keeps crap like pencils, old 8-track tapes and other stuff. I ask Pablo to tattoo La Virgen in her chola clothing on my shoulder. He's never seen her like I've seen her, so I draw a quick sketch of her.

"Hmmm," he says, looking at my drawing real close.

Can he do it? Or does he think my drawing's a piece of crap? I'll really shoot him if he tells me that. Instead, he gives me a paper cup with some yellow stuff.

"Drink it . . . a little mescal," he says.

The tattooing burns like hell, and even the mescal doesn't help. What keeps me goin' is that Pablo tells me Tía wants to teach me how to handle a needle so I can do my own tattoos, maybe work with her and Pablo here in the Templo.

"*Órale, esa*," Frida says when I tell her about Tía teaching me how to tattoo. "Let me see."

At first, I feel all proud about my crazy Virgen.

But Frida throws my arm down and growls, "What about me, *cabrona*? When the hell are you gonna put me on you?"

Fuck, I didn't know artists could get so pissy. But she's my *carnala*, and I owe her some blood. So now, I have the Virgen on my left shoulder and La Frida on my right. The next one I'm getting is the old lady I drew on the bus. She has big feathered hair and is holding her big *cuete*, almost as big as La Virgen's. She's dressed in Frida's suit and one of those old-school hats with two peaks. On her shades, you can barely see this wanna-be Pedro Infante guy she's getting ready to shoot.

"That's a *firme* tattoo, *esa*," Mousy approves.

I'm standing next to her, trying to fill in the *rebozo* on her "Adelita" tattoo. It's so hot in the salon, I'm just wearing my bra and muscle shirt. Tía doesn't care and, besides, I want to show off my tattoos.

"Is it the Virgen de Guadalupe?"

"Yeah, but she's different. See? No cutie-pie face for her."

"She's blonde?" Mousy says, like I made a mistake when I drew her.

"She's a chola, *mensa*. She's just dyed her hair, but she's still a *morena*."

Mousy moves her head closer to my shoulder. "Oh, check it out," she says. "She's wearing Dockers and everything."

"Yeah, she's one of us, a *vata loca*."

"Who did it for you?" Mousy says.

"Pablo, but I drew it first. See my picture? It's right up there, next to the jaguar. It's in the black frame next to my Frida Kahlo."

"Who's Frida Kahlo?"

"She's my *comadre*," I say. "She saved my life. See, she's on my other arm."

Mousy's my third tattoo since I started at Tía's salon. I've been working on her "Adelita" tattoo for two hours already and I'm still not finished. I have to finish her before I catch the bus to El Paso. Then I have to do my homework and get my lunch ready. Shit. I have so much to do. Plus, I need a cig. Tía won't let me smoke inside the salon because she wants to keep the place sanitary. It's not a toilet, she tells me.

The phone rings. I know it's Mom again, trying to get me to go back home. No way. She says if I don't go back home, they'll come and get me. Go ahead and try. I go back to my tattooing and forget them.

I'm trying to fill in Adelita's hair. I'm so into it, I don't hear anything except Diana Ross breathing heavily on "Love Hangover" over the speakers. Then I smell garbage and rotten meat from the butcher shop next door. I think it's Maritza who's opened the front door because she's my next appointment, and she wants a bleeding heart on her tit.

"*¡Cabrona!*"

It's Dad. He's wearing his Dodgers cap and he's standing in front of the open door. He looks half asleep, his eyes bloodshot. Don't know if it's the trip or if he's been drinking. My stomach feels real tight, and I want a cig real bad.

"Get in the car," he says, jerking his head.

Shit. Where's Frida? Where's the Virgencita?

"Who's that?" Mousy says.

"Dad."

"Motherfucker."

I see Frida walk up to my mother and lean into the car window. Mom just sits there like the car's still moving. I want La Virgen to come in and make Dad French her gun like Cowboy Dude. I want her to pop that *cuete* until teeth, blood and pieces of lip fly out of his head. But she's nowhere to be seen. Not this time. Frida's just leaning against the car, smoking a cigarette. Is she still mad about the Virgen tattoo?

"Isabela!" he says real hard.

It's like that time I put my hands up to cover my tits in the shower before he grabbed them. He walks right up to me. And I make like to ignore him and just keep working on Mousy's tattoo. I hear him suck in his breath when he sees the tattoos on my shoulders.

"*¿Me oístes, cabrona?*" he says, grabbing my hair.

I almost stab Mousy in her eye. She gets up real quick and runs to the back room.

The next thing I know, I'm drilling that needle right into his hand. He gives me a good slap on the ear as he backs off. I've still got the needle.

"Rudolfo! *¡Por Dios!*"

It's Mom. She's standing at the door with Frida and La Virgen.

"Get out," he says. "Get back in the car."

"Isabela," Mom says, wiping her red face. "He misses you."

"The only thing he misses is grabbing my tits."

I'm looking at Mom straight in the eye. Mom blinks like she doesn't understand. She's worse than a kid. More like a baby, same as Dad. She starts saying something about Tía forcing me to stay with her, changing me into some *puta* so that everybody can laugh at her. Her hands open and close, open and close.

"If anybody's gonna turn me into a *puta*, it's Dad," I say looking at him.

Dad's mouth hangs open. "*Hija de la chingada*," he says and whips off his belt.

That's when I know he's drunk, because he always acts like a *puro macho cabrón* when he gets *pedo*.

"Go ahead," I say. "I'm sick of you treating me like I'm your little whore."

"Don't say that, Isabela!" Mom cries.

Dad comes at me again. This time I grab one of those big candles, one with the picture of the Virgen, and I smash it on his head. There's glass and blood all over the place. I feel like throwing up and choking at the same time. Dad just looks at me like he doesn't know who I am. Blood drips down from all over his head to the floor.

"You're not my daughter anymore," Dad vows.

"So?"

"Don't ever come back."

"Fuckin' straight, I won't."

He reminds me of "Carrie" with all that blood covering his face. Mom just keeps crying. I can't understand what the hell she's saying. I grab another candle, just in case. . . . Mom and Dad turn and start walking out the door. They don't even look back at me.

Mousy comes up to me. She's holding my gun. I laugh because it's too late, and she's not holding it right. It's so heavy Mousy can't even lift her hand. I guess they never showed *Police Woman* down here. I stick it in her pants and cover it with the top of her shirt.

"Keep this for me, *vata*," I say. "I may need it later."

She tries to get me to the back room, but I just wanna sit down on my barber chair and watch Mom and Dad drive away. I wait for Frida and La Virgen, but I know I'm not gonna see them again for a long time. After about five minutes, I go to the door and turn over the "*abierto*" sign.

A Night of Screams in Austin, TX

Adrian Ernesto Cepeda

We sat on the couch, in Elsa's house in the middle of north Austin, passing the bong and seeing the hazy *mota* clouds hang in the air. Since there was no TV, we were all high, mesmerized and gazing at the living National Geographic special that was the glowing fish tank in the corner. Richie sat next to me.

We had driven from San Antonio to hang in his old hometown. Everywhere we went—bars, taco dives, bookstores, record shops—everyone knew Richie. I don't remember how we ended up at Elsa's house, I recall being fascinated at all the receipt tape poems hanging around the house. The poems all had themes of death and murder. The one that stood out ended with the lines:

> as I swallowed him
> on the back of the Circle K,
> with each suck of life. With
> each mouthful I tasted his little
> death muttering illicit night
> shadows screams while

shuddering as he slowly fell,
smiling almost satisfied pale
spread leaving him there
abandoned in a chalk outline
pose on concrete. As I sauntered
away, all I wanted: a Big
Gulp sip to wash down
his last sticky taste of life
out of my mouth.

As we sat stoned, Elsa kept telling us about her neighbor who had been found dead a few nights before. She was vague, purposely leaving out details. Only hinting about the knife slashes and the mysterious screams heard echoing around the neighborhood. As she spoke gleefully recreating her neighbor's last moments, we heard pounding, voices and screams coming from next door. I focused on Elsa's crazy wide dark-colored eyes. The more Elsa told us about the dead neighbor, Richie, who was the most fearless buddy I have ever known, was becoming more and more paranoid. As the pounding and voices became louder, I found myself spellbound. Elsa spoke about sneaking into the dead lady's house. "All I use is a flashlight and I let her spirit guide me. I can almost sense the aroma of silver, diamonds and gold. They whisper for me to seek them out above all the screeching howls. I am so focused on the treasures I don't even hear the screaming anymore. Not like you." Richie's eyes were panicky, something I never saw in my friend before.

"They keep finding dead animals inside the house. It's kind of cool."

The screams became quieter and then louder and the more Elsa spoke the more I was intrigued.

"I love being there in the dark, I can feel death tickle me in the dark." Richie gave me this weird, scared look, which was unlike him. Born in Australia, he was always the toughest guy in our group of buddies who played hoops. Richie was fearless. His trembling shocked me.

Elsa asked, "Do you want to sneak inside?" Maybe it was all the shots and polishing off that bottle of tequila with lime that we drank, but I didn't even have to think about it.

"Fuck yes. Let's go."

Richie had no interest in going to the dead lady's house. The screams and the hits of weed were keeping him glued to the couch. I wanted to see what the hell was next door. I gave Richie a shot of Ghost Tequila, a bottle Elsa had on the table in front of us. As he downed the Ghost, sans the worm, Elsa grabbed a flashlight, and I followed her outside. As we walked on her neighbor's lawn, we could hear cackling coming from the house.

"Here, this way," Elsa said. "We need to go in through the cellar door." I stopped. I was always fearful of cellars and basements. My older *hermanos* would lock me in the dark, so many times I would lay down on the top of the steps trying to taste the light coming from behind the basement door. I didn't want to turn around because I was no longer that little boy. I wanted to prove to myself, damn the screams, I was no longer terrified of the dark. Just hearing the cackles brought me back to those night demons, the terrors I imagined haunting me locked in the basement. I shook my head, trying to silence those voices, I didn't want to stop and ponder if they were in my imagination or waiting for me downstairs inside the house.

I could tell by the way that Richie was tugging at my shirt, he did not want us to sneak inside the dead lady's house. Elsa leaped in first, she was fearless, a natural in the darkness. I followed with Richie closely behind. With each step, I could hear noises, frightening whispers, it made me stop for a second, until I heard Elsa calling us from the bottom of the stairs, "Are you guys coming or what?" We were engulfed by darkness.

I could see spirits floating in front of our eyes, the cackling ghosts in our ears and coldness all around us. Elsa scurried off somewhere, leaving us in the middle of the room all alone.

I turned around, but Richie was no longer clutching my Rolling Stones *Tattoo You* T-shirt. "Rich, are you there?" I called out. There was nothing. I heard a rustling up ahead. Elsa had told us how the dead lady would tell her what specific treasures she wanted Elsa to take out of her house.

"Elsa, I lost Richie!" I saw a lightbulb flicker up ahead, I figured this must be where Elsa was digging for the dead lady's stuff. As I stood under the flickering lightbulb, I turned around to see if Richie was still in the basement with me. There was nothing but bursts of light, wooshes of cold air and Cucuy spirits floating around me.

Then I heard Elsa scream. She ran past me with a terrified look. "Elsa, what is it?" As I walked ahead I noticed Richie's red jacket just ahead of me. "Richie, stop playing around . . . where are you?" I walked further and as I looked inside something like a closet, I saw someone leaning against the wall. What was I going to tell his wife Bonnie? How would I explain that we snuck into a dead woman's house?

"Richie, Richie, are you okay?" When he turned to face me, it was not my friend. It was as if his jaw was trapped, stuck in midscream. He wanted to speak but I just couldn't look at his lifeless face. The one that would make me howl in laughter was a living nightmare, flashing every demon I ever imagined locked downstairs in the basement as a child. He tried chocking exhales of breaths. Like haunted cackle he could not get out. I could taste his terrifying fear. Like haunted cackle he could not get out. Just gasping, his breaths had an aroma of graveyard, worms, death; I tried turning away from Richie's pale, unnaturally contorted face frozen with fear. I had never seen him this way. His face was always tan, gutsy, full of life. Now it looked like all the blood had been sucked from his cheeks. He looked veiny, undead. I tried covering my nose, but the scent of death was overpowering, like his body had been buried and his skin was being slowly chewed up. This place had sucked out every ounce of life of the friend I no longer recognized. His once hypnotizing blue eyes that could woo any woman were dark, empty, lost and lifeless.

As I tried to find my friend, I heard an old furious woman's voice. "She traded his soul for hers. Leave him . . . he is ours." Her voice was deep, echoing and enraged that we were trespassing into her once sacred space. It was as if she was controlling the howls of agony in the basement where we were lurking.

This was when the screams started up again. Screams that surrounded me and turned into police sirens outside.

"No, not Richie. Bring him back. Not Ricardo!" This is when I started to scream, really scream, trying to hold up Richie and lead him out of the room. I felt a push. I tripped, landed in the dark. "Leave him, he belongs to us."

I imagine Elsa locking us inside. Telling the cops that the screams are a prank and that there was no one in the house. Richie fell into my arms. His corpse-like body was heavy as a coffin. It finally overpowered me and I fell. Feeling dizzy from hitting my head on the basement floor and the smell, the aroma of corpses, that surrounded the both of us, I could feel body parts, limbs, legs, dislodged arms, fingers and puddles of blood, guts squishing around me in the basement. Trying to cover my nose from the moist scent of death, I held my faint breath while slapping Richie's face. I wanted him to wake up.

Before passing out in the dark, I realized that the screams were the sounds of the other fools Elsa had led into the house, their souls trapped inside. I screamed, "ELSA . . . help us!" I felt my eyes fading, my body being sucked into the darkness. I tried to fight it but I couldn't move. I wish I had listened to Richie. I began to scream. Blood came gushing out of my mouth. Was it too late for me? Just like when my brothers had left me downstairs, the light coming from behind the door haunted me. I couldn't move. My arms were lifeless, unable to reach out as I saw the light turn off behind the door above me. I felt the darkness coming to swallow me. I wanted to call out for help. Nothing came out but pus and more blood. All I wanted was to feel some kind of light. The night shadow screams arrived instead. Whatever spirit was controlling Richie was now possessing me. I began choking on my own blood. I could no longer scream for help. I was hoping this was a bad dream and my brothers were on the other side of the door. But no one was coming to save us. I could no longer feel Richie close to me. This time I was trapped forever; there was no way out of the darkness. I just laid there, weeping bloody tears, unable to move any limbs. The painful sound of the horrifying mouth of darkness that haunted my nightmares as a child was starting to chew every inch of me. My last fading thought was, Why didn't I listen to Richie? As the agony pulsated through my limpless body, I could feel the shadow slowly devour me whole.

Indian Blood

Marcos Damián León

Nana runs her obsidian blade across her palm and allows blood to pool up, then she holds her hand above her nopales and drips blood around the roots. She closes her eyes and whispers a prayer in Nahuatl—her words bounce off the brick fence and shake my bones. Nana steps away from the nopales, her movements steady despite the cane she has to lean on, and the nopal's small buds grow into full leaves with flowers on the end.

"Córtame nopales, Luisito," she says and points to an empty strawberry box and the hoz leaning against the wall of our house. Then she moves over to the rocking chair just outside the sliding glass door. She sits down, pulls her rebozo over her thin arms, and lets out a deep breath that steams and expands against the cold air.

I grab the first nopal leaf tenderly with two fingers, careful not to touch a thorn, and cut at the base. Nana sucks her teeth at me and says, "Dale gracias a tierra."

"How am I gonna do that when you ain't taught me the prayers?" I ask and suck my teeth back at her.

She grabs a rotted tomato off her dirty-ass table and chucks it at me. I don't even gotta dodge for it to miss. Nana says, "Luis. Palabras no importan."

I roll my eyes, then I kneel beside the nopales and place my palms on the dirt around the base. "Gracias," I say, and immediately reach for the nopal leaf again.

A tomato hits my shoulder. Nana's staring at me with her lips all tight. This is what she does when she doesn't know how to say what she's thinking. Nana used to be hella talkative when Nino was still alive. She'd talk and talk at him and he'd smile and nod and translate her Nahuatl into Spanish. When he died, she tried to talk with Mom in Nahuatl, but Mom kept asking her to speak Spanish so we could understand. Now Nana stops and starts whenever she wants to talk to us, struggling to find the Spanish for what she's thinking. Me and her figured out a kinda miming language between us where she uses the Spanish she's sure of and motions the rest for me. Nana points to the nopales and says, "En serio." I groan. My whining echoes off the bricks and makes me sound like a little bitch. Nana laughs. I put my palms to the dirt around the nopales, close my eyes, and breathe out. Nothing changes: I don't feel anything in me, or from the nopales or dirt. Nana holds her hands to her chest in a ball above her heart, then moves them towards the nopales. "Dale gracias. Por todo," Nana whispers.

We do this every week: I wake up hella early, before sunrise, and find her out back, kneeling in the center of the empty dirt plot that makes up our backyard, then, I take my place beside her and we give thanks to the rising sun, her in Nahuatl and me in broken Spanish, and, once she says that the Sun and tierra are happy with us, I follow her around the yard as she bleeds onto crops she's cared for my whole life. Nopales and tomatoes and tomatillos and maize and chiles have their spots along the red brick fence—when I was a chiquillo, the whole yard was filled with rows of crops that Nana would care for after working the lettuce fields. She'd sell those crops as a side hustle, but her body is too drained to keep feeding this many plants. Now, she only keeps enough to make our dinner. I wish she didn't have to keep any plants at all. I should be able to take care of her.

"Thank you for taking care of us all these years," I say, and for the first time in my life, I mean it. These plants have done so much for us—a thank you is the least I could give them, and, really, I want to give them more.

The dirt pulses against my palms. I jump, my heart racing. The nopales grow upwards and outwards a bit more. "Did I do that?" I ask Nana and point at the nopales. She nods. The plants ain't ever responded to me. I see them grow with Nana's blood, but they've never given a damn about me. When I was in middle school I pricked my finger and begged a rose bush to give me a flower for this cute morenita in my class, but, no matter how much I bled or cried, the rose didn't grow. Since then I've been convinced that there's some prayer Nana's hiding since she won't teach me Nahuatl.

"Ahora sí. Córtalos," she says. I look at her then the nopales, then back and forth, which seems to annoy her, cause she puckers her lips to point at the hoz.

I kneel beside the nopal again and take the leaf between my fingers: The outer skin is cold, but I feel a deeper warmth—like when I caress Nana's tired hands. The nopal is alive. It knows me. My pulse throbs in my fingers. I blink and the world starts to spin. My hand grows hotter. I snatch it away and try to stand, but I'm dizzy.

"No des mucho," Nana says.

I cut off each of the new leaves, holding them only for a second, and lay them flat in the strawberry box. I finish cutting all the leaves. Exhaustion radiates out from my hands. My eyes are heavy. My breathing is slow. I feel like I could lay down and sleep even though I just got up.

I shake my head and ask Nana, "We growing anything else?"

She shakes her head. We haven't grown anymore in over a week though, but, based on how I'm feeling, she's way too tired to feed the plants more of herself. Nana ain't that old: Mom had me when she was sixteen and Nana had her when she was fifteen, so, since I'm turning nineteen soon, that means Nana's only fifty, even if she looks and moves like she's seventy. She's given too much of herself to the lettuce fields.

I help her up and put my arms under her armpits, to hold half her weight as she walks inside, past the dim living room with an altar to La Virgen de Guadalupe surrounded by faded pictures of long-gone family, and, finally, to the kitchen. She sits at her chair at the end of the dining table. I go back outside and bring her the box of nopales. Then I run back to the room I share with Tío Chuy and Pepito and change into my blue jeans, grey polo and McDonald's cap. When I come back out, Nana is already cutting the thorns off the nopales with her old-chipped knife. "I gotta go work," I tell her.

"Ven," she says and motions me toward her. I lean down so our faces are level. She rubs two fingers of her right hand on the same palm, now covered in dried blood, then reaches up and rubs those bloodied fingers on my forehead. She whispers something I don't understand. I try to stand, but she pulls my head down. Nana makes the sign of the cross, motions from my forehead to chest and shoulders, and says, "Dios te proteja."

"Why you bless me with old shit and then Jesus?" I ask her.

"Más safe," she says. I suck my lips, which is a mistake cause I'm close enough that she smacks me upside my head.

I rub my head all exaggerated to make her feel bad, but she goes back to her nopales. "I'll see you later, Nana," I say and walk to the front door. She grunts in response.

Our house is only a twenty-minute walk from the McDonalds I work at. We live right down the street from Closter Park, the neighborhood where most of the field workers live.

"What up, cuh?" Kiko calls to me as I walk in front of his house, his accent weirdly natural and fake all at once. Usually he wears a fancy suit to work—that combined with his blonde e-boy fluffy hair make him look hella outta place—but he's sitting on a chair on his porch in his LA Chicano outfit with the fucking Dickies shorts, flannel and knee socks.

"Heading to work, bruh," I say. He's kinda weird, like that tío that thinks he's still young, but we've always been cool.

"Still flipping burgers?" he says pushing back his long blonde hair and smiling in a way that means he thinks he's being funny.

"Not everyone lucky enough to have a white boy job," I say, but immediately regret it. He's always talking about Chicano this and that, so that might've crossed the line.

He laughs though. Which feels worse than any threat he coulda made. He licks his lips and says, "What other job could get me all my nice shit?" Everyone in our neighborhood is Mexican, but that don't mean we're the same. Kiko's got money: He went to college and came back to work for some fancy business in that new building on the Southside. Every other house around here looks old—they're owned by fuckers who pack them full of farmworkers or people who can't afford to eat and fix their house—but Kiko's house got brand new everything, from a silly white picket fence to new cars in the driveway for him and his girl.

Kiko stands up from his chair and walks across his lawn. He doesn't stop till he's right in front of me, so close I feel his breath on my face. "I hear you and your grams out in the yard sometimes," he says, quiet enough that I know he wants to keep this conversation on the low. "I see how her plants grow. You know how she does it?"

"Yeah," I respond before really thinking about it. Like, yeah, I know the steps, but I have no idea what made the nopales respond to me this morning.

"I got a business idea. Could make hella money. I need one of you real-ass *indios* though," he says and puts his hand on my shoulder. I want to shrug him off but his grip is tight. "My family? We're old Aztecs. Straight from Tenochtitlan, but the Spanish stole our language from us. Fucked us up real bad. Your grams? She's from some middle of nowhere pueblo where they got to keep the language. She knows stuff that could save all us Chicanos from these fucking gringos. If she passed that down to you, I could give you work."

Nana warned me to stay away from Kiko. She says his family has always been bad: Kiko's dad was a drug dealer who got put away for murder, and not even Kiko's UCLA degree and fancy job can wash away his family's sins—so Nana blesses the fence between our houses to keep us safe.

"What they pay you?" he asks and puts my McDonalds hat on for me.

"Fourteen an hour," I say.

Kiko grabs his wallet, pulls out a hundred-dollar bill, and puts it in my hand. "This is a gift. Lot more if you take my job. Think about it." He walks back to his porch. I watch him, waiting for him to say more, but he don't even look at me.

I keep going toward McDonalds. The beat-up houses turn into beat-up apartments. Once I get to Williams Road, there are more cars full of people driving their kids to school or themselves to work. I walk past the smelly laundromat that spills dirty water onto the street as cars *honk-honk-honk*.

"Clean the bathroom, then go sweep outside," Ms. Joana says as soon as I walk in the restaurant. She's never liked me, but she's really on my ass lately.

"Yes, ma'am," I say. There's no point arguing. She's always got something to say about employees needing to work efficiently and show her respect.

I grab the bucket of cleaning supplies, with the broom and mop, and go to the bathroom. The bathroom's not that bad: Some new tags on the stall and toilet paper on the floor. Whatever. I pull some gloves on, wipe the mirrors and stall walls, brush the urinal and toilet, sweep and mop and put out the wet floor sign before doing the same in the women's bathroom.

When I come out, there's a line of people in the restaurant and a line of cars in the drive thru. We're always busy early on 'cause Ms. Joana fired Tony for being five minutes late and refuses to hire anyone, but these lines are longer than usual. Joey is taking the drive thru orders and Dani is preparing stuff in the back. No one's helping the people inside. Whatever. Ms. Joana gets mad if we do stuff our way instead of following orders, so I grab the outside broom and start sweeping. I sweep the sidewalks all around the restaurant, the outside eating area, and grab a bucket to pick up the big trash nearby.

Then a younger güera in nurse's scrubs comes up to me and says, "Can you come take our orders?" She points inside, where the line is wrapping around one of the tables.

I smile at her and say, "Yes, ma'am."

I leave my bucket and walk inside with her. I take all the orders—the güera is at the end of the line.

"Thanks for your patience," I tell her.

She leans over the counter, reads my name tag and says, "Luis. You can get me your manager."

I imitate her as I read her name tag and respond, "Araceli, you don't gotta do all that."

"Yeah, I do," she says.

"Let me just get your order and we can get you your food," I tell her with the biggest smile I can force. Some people are shit, but I need to put up with everything for this paycheck. We've been struggling since Nana stopped working—it's hard to keep up with the rent on the house and her diabetes treatments since we don't have health insurance.

"Go get your manager," she says again, this time with her hands on her hips and that Karen voice that means she wants to feel important. The other people who were in line don't seem interested in Nurse Karen's little tantrum, which is probably for the best.

"I'll be right back," I say with a smile. I walk to the little office where Ms. Joana sits and hides from customers and all her workers, and tell her, "A woman wants to talk to you." She sighs real loud and gets up slow.

Ms. Joana follows me to the front and asks Nurse Karen, "How can I help you, ma'am?" in her soft voice that sounds like she's one bad day away from crying on the floor in her office.

Nurse Karen hits her back with the exact same tone and says, "This man kept us waiting while he swept outside." It's wild how white ladies all got this act down: Right now they're both at level one, like they feel kinda bad about something; next level is the one Ms. Joana uses on angry Mexican dudes where she physically shrinks; and the last level is full-on crying and screaming. This don't seem serious enough for anything past level one.

Ms. Joana's tired white lady act breaks just for a second so she can shoot me a scowl, then she's immediately back to her performance: "I'm so sorry, ma'am. I'll make sure your order gets out immediately."

Nurse Karen goes from angry watery eyes to blinking away confusion and she says, "Well, I haven't ordered actually—"

"I'll take your order now then," Ms. Joana says, switching from tired white lady act to helpful manager. As good as Nurse Karen is with the sad white lady shit, Ms. Joana is a goddamn expert at manipulating situations until she's in control.

Nurse Karen seems confused for a second, but orders her fucking McChicken anyways. I'm stuck standing there, waiting for Ms. Joana to tell me whatever the hell she's gonna say after that mess. Ms. Joana turns to me, glaring, and, in her same helpful manager voice says, "Can you go get these people their orders?"

I head back and Dani already got the first order bagged and ready. I take it up, call the number and leave it on the counter so Ms. Joana doesn't glare at me for standing around. I take up each order as soon as Joey finishes them, and, when all the customers are gone, I tell Ms. Joana, "Thanks for backing me up."

"Luis, you're fired," she says as casually as if she were talking about the weather. It takes me a second to remember that this is no-bullshit Ms. Joana and I reel it in.

"Wait—"

"You're fired," she says again.

"Oh shit," Joey whispers from the drive-thru window with the headset still on.

My first instinct is to promise I'll do better and explain that I need the money to take care of my Nana and that I've been a good consistent worker for three years, then it hits me that maybe I don't need this job. Kiko offered me work. He gave me a hundred bucks like it was nothing. Maybe I have another option.

"Okay," I say. Her composure breaks and for the first time since I started working here she looks confused. She can't threaten me or control the situation when I don't care about whatever power she has. "Make sure I get my last check," I say, pull off my McDonald's cap and leave it on the counter.

"Wait—" she starts to say something but I don't hear the rest of it after the door closes behind me. I wanna have the last word. I want her to remember that when it came down to it, I stood up for myself.

I stop by the Rite Aid at the corner of the shopping center and use the money Kiko gave me to buy Nana one of the cute little potted plants they keep out front with the bright orange flowers, and, since I'm in there anyway, I get myself some Hot Cheetos. Then I walk out the store and just take in the sky: It's that nice baby blue with white fluffy clouds extending into the horizon. The sun is warm on my face and there's the smallest breeze, which is the best we can hope for in Salinas at the end of winter. Right now, I understand exactly why rich old fucks move to this area to retire: The weather is perfect, the air feels good in my lungs and, goddamn, if I don't gotta work a shit job I might actually get to go to those pretty-ass beaches and hiking trails that the kids with money were always talking about. I just gotta talk to Kiko and figure out how to get enough money so that Nana can live good like the rich old fucks on the Southside.

I take my time walking home, but it's still early when I get to our street.

"Done flipping burgers, cuh?" Kiko asks from his porch chair—he hasn't moved since I walked by on my way to work.

"I got fired," I say.

Kiko laughs loud enough that the birds sitting in the trees around us fly off. "For real?" he asks.

"Yeah," I tell him.

"What's the plan now?" he asks.

"You offered me a job, right? How much you paying?"

Kiko stands up and walks across his yard to stand in front of me. "How much you want?"

The McDonald's job was paying me fourteen an hour and only giving me six hours a day so we wouldn't get benefits. With my parents, my tío and Pepito, and me, paying the bills should be easy, but, between sending money back to Mexico and covering Nana's medical bills and the landlord raising our rent, it's never enough. "I want one-fifty for a day of work," I say. That's almost double what I was making at McDonalds.

Kiko laughs again, then, he holds out his hand and says, "Deal." We shake. Kiko walks over to his truck. "Let's go. I'ma show you what we're doing," he says and climbs in.

Nana says that we gotta speak our intentions into the world to ask for our ancestors' blessing. "I'll do what he wants so I can take care of Nana. I can do this. I'm strong enough. I have to be," I say. I open up my bag of Hot Cheetos and drop a few on the ground—I hope the ancestors like them as much as I do cause it's the only offering I got on me.

I climb into the passenger seat of Kiko's Silverado. He puts on some garbage Chicano rap and drives us out past the shopping center and Alisal High School, past even the new housing on the edge of town, toward Old Stage Road on the edge of the mountains. Out here there's only lettuce fields.

Kiko says, "My abuela used to tell me stories about indios who still prayed to Aztec gods. She said that my bisabuela was full-on Aztec and could grow plants by feeding them blood. When I went to UCLA, I learned about Chicano history and realized that shit's our heritage. Curanderismo and all that." He uses the break and points out the windshield, toward the fields, and asks, "You know why the farmworkers leave for Yuma in the winter?"

We're driving slow at the foot of the mountain. The winter rains were good this year so the mountainside is covered in grass so green it looks like gross neon candy. To our right are empty lettuce fields—there's a couple farmworkers scattered across them, but it'll be another few weeks before their colorful sweaters make a kaleidoscope outta the valley floor.

"It's too cold to grow shit here," I say, unsure why he's asking something so obvious.

"So what if we gave them a way to grow crops even when it's cold?" he asks.

"I can't maintain an entire field on my own," I say. Even when Nana was younger she could only feed our backyard, so there's no way I could do a whole field.

Kiko turns to me, takes his eyes fully off the road, and says "We ain't got a deal if you can't do the job."

"I could teach other people," I say without thinking.

Kiko scrunches up his eyes in confusion. "Don't they gotta be indios?"

"No," I say and think about this morning. The plants responded to me after years—what changed? The only thing I can think of is that I treated them like people, like the family that they are. "They just gotta believe," I say.

Kiko turns onto to the road, leans back and puts his knees on the wheel to steer. "Okay, so, here's the thing," he says, moving his hands as he talks. "I known bout you and your grams for a bit. I knew there was money in it. Growing and selling weed ain't worth it cause of the dispensaries. Plus, the fucking licenses are so expensive only Elon Musk can afford that shit." He turns to look at me. I nod. "So I'm driving out here, just tryna unwind after a hard day at the office, and it hits me. Look at all this land! These fuckers want to squeeze it dry, so what if we help them?" He holds his hands out in front of him, palms up, eyes looking to Heaven—the same pose used to pray to Jesucristo.

"We can do it if you get people for me to teach," I say.

"You gotta do it yourself," Kiko says. I can feel anger evaporating off his skin—sweat collects on my face and back despite the stubborn cold and threatening winds. There's a tension pulling his body: His eyes seem almost magnetically focused on the road, the muscles on his arms and neck are flexed, and his jaw is pushing out so his face looks like a damn bike seat. "I lost some money in a bad investment. I might lose my house," he says and looks at me. There's anger there, but a deep sadness too. "Both our families need this money."

"I've never tried to grow a whole field by myself, but, if you help me, maybe we can make it work," I say. The rest of the drive, I'm focused on the connection I felt this morning. I need to let my consciousness sink into the ground and connect my body to the plants. I need to offer them pieces of myself and treat them with the respect I would another person. After twenty minutes, we turn onto a small dirt road that leads to a sectioned-off field surrounded by tall bushy trees that block the wind. The field is smaller than I expected, barely even the same as two football fields sitting next to each other, but, even then, it's still a huge plot for me to maintain on my own.

Kiko stops at the end of the dirt road. He gets out of the truck and motions for me to join him. The small field looks like our backyard: An empty dirt plot that's been used to grow crops, but now lies empty and dead. "What do you think?" Kiko asks. He's already got the field prepared with more rows than I can count, each one extending further than I can see.

Only the trees around the field remind me that it's not endless—no matter how huge it feels from the edge.

"What kinda plants are those?" I ask him, pointing to the close end of the field where small plants fill a couple rows. We walk closer: The plants have long sharp leaves such a light color of green that they're basically white.

"White sage," he says. After his big explanation, I expected some fancy boujee food. I guess he sees my confusion, 'cause he says, "California Indians use it to smudge."

"Smudge?"

"What kinda indio are you?" he asks. I'm about to answer but he holds a hand up. "Has your grams ever burned a plant to get rid of spirits?" I nod. "That's smudging. Gringo hippies and wannabe witches are really into that shit. They pay out the ass for white sage, but they're making the plant go extinct. I talked to some shop owners in Carmel and Pacific Grove and told them I could get ethical white sage bundles. We gonna be selling a little stick of leaves for forty a pop."

"Sounds kinda stupid," I say.

Kiko pushes his blonde hair outta his face and says, "Gringos tryna exorcise the evil spirits in their lives like it's not their murdering colonizer ancestors." He laughs at his own joke, so forcefully that I shiver.

I kneel down and touch the closest plant's leaves: They're shriveled and black at the edges. "The cold is killing these plants," I tell Kiko. "I don't think there's any saving them."

Kiko white knuckles his fists. The anger from earlier shakes his body. For a second, I'm sure that he's about to swing at me, but he just lets out a deep sigh. "You're the only one who can do this, primo," he says. The way he says it, his voice soft and steady like the morning birds calling out to each other with the sunrise, hopeful that their friends made it through the night too, makes my fear and doubt melt away. Nana always said that what she does is share her energy with the tierra and plants and they return it; and, in this moment, Kiko is pouring his energy into me and trusting me to return it.

"Okay," I say.

Kiko nods and says, "Thank you."

We drive back home in silence. We park in front of Kiko's house and he tells me, "Be out here at six tomorrow morning."

It's dark by the time I walk in my house, but no one's car is back yet—Mom and Dad are still at the salad packing plant and Tío Chuy and Pepito are still out in the fields. I find Nana in the backyard, her thickest rebozo wrapped around her body.

I sit on the dirt next to her chair and ask, "How do I make the plants grow?"

"Tú sabes," she says, except, I don't know. This morning the plants stretched out like they were letting out a little yawn, but when I go back to Kiko's field I'm gonna need those plants to grow tall.

"How do I get them to grow like you?" I ask.

She sucks her teeth at me and repeats, "Tú sabes." I groan. She smacks the back of my head. I turn to look at her: She's looking up at the sky, like the Spanish words she's looking for might be up there somewhere. Nana holds her hands to her chest, opens her arms outwards and says, "Dale energía."

I understand that part, but I don't know how to teach that to someone like Kiko. I kneel in front of Nana and say, "Gimme your hands." She puts them palm up, on her thighs. I take her right hand in mine, softly run my thumb down the calluses that run from the base of her fingers to the tips, then I run my four fingers across the still healing cut on her palm.

"No duele," she says and smiles.

The skin around the cut is as thick as the calluses—her body gave up hope that it wouldn't be hurt again a long time ago, so now it raises the flesh for her to cut, presenting a small spot that can be hurt if only to save the rest of her body. I rub her hands, careful to not disturb her scars. "I want to be able to grow the plants so you don't have to," I tell her.

She takes my face in her hands and says, "Dale amor."

I'm dressed in some old boots, jeans, a hoodie and a thick jacket at 5:40 a.m. Nana's in the backyard already, so I go out there and tell her that I have to go open for work today. She motions for me to kneel next to her and blesses me, "Qué Dios te bendiga." I give her a hug, pocket her obsidian knife when she turns away and head out. Kiko's already waiting in his truck.

I climb into the passenger seat. Kiko's wearing some old jeans, muddy boots and a new-looking Carhart jacket—it's like a costume that's too big for him. He smiles and says, "Let's do this."

We drive out through the neighborhood and the edges of East Salinas. There ain't any other cars on the street and the sun won't be up for another hour, so it feels like a ghost town. A shiver runs through me and prickles my arms. I pull my jacket tighter even though Kiko's got the heat on—Nana says that goosebumps happen when our ancestors try to talk to us: Since we can't hear them, all they can do is set off something in our body like an alarm. I look out at the streets for someone watching us, or a cop or anything that might mean we're in trouble. There's no one out there, at least no one I can see.

We turn into the tree surrounded field. We park in the same spot, at the edge closest to the white sage.

I grab Nana's obsidian knife outta my pocket, then run the blade across my palm, let the blood pool up and drip the blood around the roots of the closest plant, just like Nana does. I place my hands on the ground around the sage, feeling the cut on my hand burn against the cold air, close my eyes and pray. I think back to the day that the plants responded to me: All I could think about was the years and years that those plants had fed us and helped keep a roof over our heads, and, even though these plants are young, I know they can do the same. "Please accept my blood, my offering, and help me take care of my Nana. I'll take care of you and make sure that you live as long as I do." I let my thoughts sink down into the dirt with my blood, hoping that each drop carries my prayers for a good life and my promises of care. I breathe in. Out. The dirt pulses against my hands. "Thank you," I whisper. I open my eyes and the sage's leaves grow two, three, then four times bigger. The stalks in the middle of the plant grow tall, with new stems covered in leaves shooting off in every direction. I smile and look up at Kiko.

He whistles, then says, "Holy shit." He walks back to his truck and comes back to me with a crop box, the kind that bunches of vegetables get packaged in. He pulls out a long knife and cuts leaves off the plant, bunching them together with thick twine.

"I told you I could do it," I say. Something changed this week, maybe it's just the way I see things now, but I got a whole-ass plant to grow the way Nana does. I can do this. I can take care of Nana and make sure she never has to hurt herself to feed me again.

"What are you waiting for?" Kiko asks and nods down the row of plants. "We not getting rich off one plant, no matter how much the gringos pay."

I nod and move down the row. Each time I repeat my prayer as best I can: I drip my blood around the root of the plant, place my hands to the dirt, pray for a good life and promise to care for the plant. Each plant takes a couple minutes to pray over and grow. It's not the physical action though, it's just the connection between me and the plant. Each plant is different and decides itself how much blood and prayer it needs before it accepts my promises of care and grow. If one plant takes too long, I need to recut my hand—shallow enough that I don't bleed wastefully, but deep enough that I can offer myself to the plants. By the end of the first row, only about a dozen plants, the cut on my hands hurts and I'm feeling tired. I don't give each plant much blood, but it's adding up to make me lightheaded.

"Can you try for the next plant?" I ask Kiko.

"Why?" he asks from down the row where he's picking leaves off the third plant.

"Man, I'm a little dizzy. You know, I'm offering up my blood each time," I say and show him my palm. The skin around the cut is bright pink, and the cut, even if it's shallow and thin, is starting to swell up.

Kiko drops his box and walks close enough that I can see the irritated pink on his nose from the cold. "You said that to learn I have to believe the plants are alive? Like they think and shit? I don't. You have to do it," he says and shrugs.

I look around me: Even the first time out here this seemed like an impossible field to care for by myself, but I thought if I took it a step at a time, like telling myself only fifteen more minutes over and over for every full shift and McDonalds, that I could handle it all. Now though, I'm at the end of the first row and I'm not sure my body can offer much more to the plants around me. The last couple of sage plants have been smaller than the first ones, too, so I know the plants can tell I've got less to give. "I'm not doing this shit alone," I tell Kiko.

"That's not good enough," Kiko yells. His shout echoes in the clearing. Birds fly outta the trees around us. Goosebumps explode on my arms. Kiko's nose twitches. His whole body shakes with anger. He balls up his fists, closes his eyes and breathes so heavy that his shaking vibrates the air. "I need this money," he says. "I didn't tell you the whole truth. My wife threatened to leave me. I'm gonna lose everything."

"I can't do this alone," I yell back at him. I don't like to get mad cause it feels like it poisons everything I do, but I can't stand Kiko thinking I'm going to hurt myself to save his ass.

"Look," Kiko continues, "We had a deal. You come out here and grow these plants for me and I pay you one-fifty a day. If you don't grow the damn plants, I'm not paying you."

"I already grew this whole row," I say through gritted teeth.

"That's business, primo. I'm paying you to do a job, so do it," he says, walks back to his box and goes back to cutting and wrapping bundles of sage.

"I need the money," I say again. My family can maybe make it a week without my paychecks. Maybe. I could get another fast-food job pretty quick, but I'd end up in the exact same spot: Making shit money for some shitty manager and a shitty job, and Nana would still have to hurt herself everyday to feed us. "I need this job," I tell Kiko.

"Then get back to work," he says.

I press Nana's obsidian blade into my hand, let the blood pool up, bleed on the dirt around the plant, place my hands around the base of the next sage plant and pray. I pray for a better life. I pray for Nana's health. I pray for food. The white sage hears me each time. It grows tall. I move to the next plant, then the next. I look up and the whole clearing spins around me. I shake my head. Move to the next plant. I bleed. I pray. The sage grows as tall as a building. I shake my head and the plant shrinks down to my height. The trees around me dance. I move to the next plant, cutting my hand again so that I can keep bleeding for the sage—so I can keep bleeding for Kiko. He's behind me in the row. Cutting the leaves that I bled for. I pray and bleed and the world around me spins.

I fall to the ground. Everything spinning. Darkness at the edge of my vision. Kiko looks at me. Rage in his eyes. Contempt. "Get your ass up and keep moving," he says. He's using me just like Ms. Joana. I cut my hand. I bleed on the white sage. I pray for Kiko to suffer.

The plants grow. They absorb my rage. Roots grow at Kiko's feet. They grab at his boots. He kicks his feet free. Stumbles backwards and falls. The roots reach up around his body—impossibly small hands tryna catch him. Kiko sits up and rips away the roots around his legs. "What the fuck?" he screams. He looks at me, and all that's left in his eyes is fear. "Primo, come on. Stop this shit. I'll pay you more. I'll help with the plants. Just show me."

The white sage is louder. I can feel its thoughts: It asks me for more. More energy. More anger. More blood.

I press my bleeding hand flat against the base of the white sage and say, "Take it all."

The roots wrap around Kiko's legs. He tries to cut them off, but they grow back twice as thick. They spring out of the ground, catch Kiko's body and slam him flat on his back. He screams. The roots grow thicker. "I'll give you all the money I got. Please. Let me go," Kiko says, his words muffled by tears, roots and dirt. The roots pull him under. His screaming fades and stops. I feel my own laughter echo in the clearing. The distant trees shake and laugh with me.

My hands are still pressed against the now giant white sage. It's hungry. Its roots tenderly wrap around my hands and insert into my veins. The white sage and I are connected. It's too cold in this valley. It needs my help to survive. It needs my energy. The world spins and spins and spins so that I have to close my eyes. Just for a second. The dark of my eyes spins too so I lay down. Just for a minute. The cold fades away. The spinning stops.

Detached

Leticia Urieta

The storm wails outside, creaking the trees against the window. I lie in bed, trying to sleep against the noise and the shadows. Pressure builds in my face from the pull of the storm. Pain is familiar, but sharper tonight, cresting in waves, drawing me under. I feel the pull in the left cheek, right under my eye, a hook caught in my meat and reeling me in. And it does. The storm pulls and pulls until my left side begins to separate along my spine like paper torn along a perforated edge.

It doesn't hurt as much as I thought it would, the separation. My organs don't come spilling from me onto the bed. Instead, my body unzips and I can no longer feel my left arm or leg or the normal ache in my hip from lying on that side.

My left side gets up to stand at the window, pressing my hand against the rain-splattered glass. I can still see out of that eye. The Left Me looks into the darkness, sees our reflection in the glass. They open the window, wind whipping the rain inside, and jump out on the muddy ground a story below. I watch all of this from the bed, and in my mind I can see what Left Me sees in a cloudy dream.

Left Me is buffeted by the storm outside, but doesn't seem to have trouble balancing as they glide down the street, a perfect, perforated ghost. A natural healer once told me during a pain reduction massage that the left side of the body is the most sensitive part, the part that receives energy and processes pain. As she rubbed her elbow into the tender flesh of my left shoulder, she explained how she was trying to release the tension, the pain, the residual trauma that was stored in the muscles and bundles of nerves on my left side. When I left the massage, I iced my shoulder and wondered if what she said was true. What was she unlocking, her hands on my body?

Left Me moves like a corporeal shadow down the street. The me that remains lies immobilized on the bed like I have been so many times, but now the source of my pain has left me. They move and move against the wind with intent. I feel their being full of the bitter bile of rage and waiting. They fly past houses, past our neighborhood and to another part of the city I have never been to before where tall, two-story white houses with long columns and wide lawns crowd the street. They move to the front steps of one house with red curtains in the window and the lights gleaming in the rain. They knock on the door once, twice, three and four times, pounding over the storm, and I realize, as they already know, that this is my doctor's house, the woman I hadn't been to see in six months after she denied me the pain medication I needed, after my insurance lapsed and I couldn't pay. She whips open the door in a frenzy, her black and gray hair silhouetted against the tan of her face. Left Me stands on the bottom step. At first, the doctor doesn't know what she is seeing. Her eyes widen and she covers her mouth as Left Me stretches wide their half mouth and vomits dark red blood and bile onto her pristine brick steps. They seem to have a whole stomach full even though they are only half of me, and I watch through Left Me's eye as they grin with bloody teeth at the doctor and skulk away into the darkness, the doctor screaming into the swallow of the wind.

Suddenly, we are soaring above the city, over skyscrapers and through damp clouds. When Left Me lands again, they are in front of a weather-worn apartment building with peeling blue paint. There are rose bushes on either side of building number four, and Left Me bends down to wrench the largest crimson bloom off by the stem, their fingers pricking on the short thorns. They walk up to the apartment on the ground floor, 409, and knock. Back in bed, I cringe to remember this door, how long it has been since I've last stood in front of it with gifts of wine and cheese in hand as an offering. It takes eight echoing knocks for my friend, who I haven't seen in over a year, really since my official diagnosis, to open the door, bleary eyed and blinking. She has shaved her hair on the left side and colored the right bangs a vivid pink, which I admire but can't compliment her on. At first she recognizes me, and smiles a cautious, worried smile because Left Me stands in shadow, and she tries to invite me inside with all her generous heart, but when she opens the door wider, light from her apartment falls onto my face and she sees the whole gruesome picture of Left Me standing on her step, offering her a rose speckled with blood. As Left Me leans toward her with the rose, it bursts into orange and blue flames. They let the light illuminate my friend's shocked pale face, then throw the charring flower onto her doormat that reads, "Welcome to the Den of Mischief." We don't stay long enough to see if the mat, or perhaps the entire building catches fire.

The rain is coming down in drips now but Left Me continues to shift and fly against the wind on their bizarre ritual.

The last stop on their parade I know before they even land. The beige, weathered duplex is familiar to me, especially in the dark, the times I have usually been asked to leave. Left Me lands near the window to my lover's room. The window is cracked open to let the cool, rainy air in, so they push it up the rest of the way and slide inside. My lover sleeps undisturbed. It's been a few weeks since I last spent the night here. We never spent more than a few nights together at a time; he worked long hours and I had graduate classes, but one weekend we took a trip to the beach. The first day was full of luxurious sex, rolling waves and a shrimp dinner on a wood patio overlooking the ocean, but by the second day I was in bed, a pain in my left temple throbbing. I wished I was home with my extra strength medications and tinctures, my blackout curtains and soft lighting, and most of all I wished to hide my pain away from him before it infected our time together. He tried to comfort me in all the most ineffectual ways, and when he saw he couldn't help, he became frustrated at the waste of a trip and took me home early.

My counterpart watches him tucked safely in his bed while his lips hang open in a wheezing snore. After a while, they stalk to the bathroom and turn on the light. I can see us now like a reflection of infinite selves, both the room around me and their bloody, frenzied reflection. My frizzy curls halo my half-self and my bright green eye is wide with wonder. Left Me leans their forehead and temple against the frigid glass with all the relief of a cool salve. While my lover sleeps, they smash the mirror with my left hand which has become dominant and more powerful than I've ever seen. They go through the house smashing mirrors, there are three altogether, and collecting them in the small bowl of my ragged black T-shirt. Floating back into the bedroom, Left Me arranges the shards now smeared with more blood in a mosaic halo around my lover's sleeping head where his silky, long, blond hair sweeps the pillow. He never stirs except to smile in his sleep, looking so much like an oblivious baby or a broken angel.

Left Me returns hours later, dripping wet and covered in mud and flecks of blood. They lay back down next to me on the bed and turn to face the rest of me, their smile gleaming in the moonlight. They run a muddy hand through my black hair on the pillow, press cold fingers to their lips, then to mine like they are tucking me in tenderly, the way a mother would, though ours was never so tender. They turn onto their back in submission, allowing me to scoot closer and rejoin them, our bodies knitting themselves back together along my skin, shoulder muscles rejoining muscles, lips rejoining swollen lips. When we are one again, I don't move to wash myself. My hands run along my chest, my pelvis and legs to be sure that all of me is back together. The pain and pressure have subsided to a distant ache behind my left eye, a whisper from seeing for the first time.

I turn on my right side, away from the tenderness of my left temple, and stare out the window, because the moon is bright and nothing has changed.

Purveyors and Puppets

Pedro Iniguez

Once she'd entered the sanctuary of her home and fastened the bolts on the door, Anna pressed her face against the window. The street was empty save for the throngs of moths hovering over the flickering light of the lamp posts.

She drew the blinds shut. Four months hadn't put enough distance between her and the stalker hellbent on silencing her "liberal howling." The police weren't even sure how he'd acquired her address.

Anna ran a hand along the back of her neck, massaging the tightly wound coils of muscle. Her fingers glided toward her throat. She felt the raised scar tissue where the knife had sliced her flesh. A carefully placed elbow to his solar plexus and a short run to the neighbor's house had saved her. Thankful couldn't begin to describe how she'd felt escaping with her life that night.

She poured herself a glass of wine and settled into the couch, flipping through TV channels until she found what she was looking for.

The woman on the screen looked back at her through fiery brown eyes as she waxed poetic about the wave of police brutality disproportionately afflicting people of color. Anna's producers told her that she needed to smile more, that a perceived warmth would draw in more viewers. God knew she needed them. After she got out of the hospital, she had the number one show on TV. For two weeks. But as all ratings eventually did, they had started to slide. She chuckled. No. Her issue wasn't smiling, it was finding out who was lighting the show, because God knew she looked like a pale corpse under those lights.

"Join us tomorrow as we invite councilman Robert Tao to discuss his push toward expanding voting rights in his district, the poorest in the state."

Her mobile rang. Anna nearly fumbled her glass. Restricted number. Again. She let it ring.

"Thank you for tuning in to Liberal Lioness," the TV version of herself said, "I'm your host, Anna Acevedo."

Anna looked at her glass and found herself staring back from a pool of sloshing crimson. Her eyes appeared sunken-in, dark. All those sleepless nights. Maybe it wasn't the lighting but the dread that someone had been watching from the shadows. Another fanatic who didn't take kindly to immigrant TV show hosts.

The phone rang again.

Screw it, she thought, and picked up.

"Hello, Ms. Acevedo?" a soft-spoken woman on the line said.

"I'm sorry, who is this?" Anna downed the wine.

"Sorry to call so late. My name is Dakota Ellsworth, I'm a producer on The Daily Roundup with Kirk Sullivan."

"That right-wing asshole?"

"Correct," Ellsworth said.

"Why are you calling me?" Anna said, wondering how they'd gotten her number.

"We'd like to invite you onto the show tomorrow evening. We know it's last minute, but Mr. Sullivan has requested your appearance. He values your opinions."

"Bullshit," Anna said. "He's been taking shots at me since I premiered last year. Some of his viewers have taken his message to heart, as I'm sure you know." She swore she could feel the scar on her throat begin to throb.

"Network chest-puffing. Spectacle. Grabbing for ratings, as you know. Personally, he finds your point-of-view refreshing and engaging. He even admires your story. Immigrant who made her own way in this country? Nothing short of the American Dream."

Anna didn't respond.

"You'll be compensated," Ellsworth said. "And it'll be a fair discussion. Our show boasts the highest evening news ratings so your appearance could offer your own program a boost."

Ellsworth wasn't wrong. Critics, bloggers, die-hard liberals; they'd all tune in just to see what the fuss was about. Higher ratings meant a longer contract and a larger platform. After a long pause she sighed and said, "Okay, I'll do it."

"Wonderful," Ellsworth said. She filled Anna in on the details and thanked her for her time.

What would her producers think? That she was being led into an ambush, surely. *Damn*. But would they also think it was worth the risk?

Anna put her hand over her eyes. She'd been so tired she forgot to ask what they'd be discussing. A woman's right to complete bodily autonomy? Or perhaps immigration and the influx of "parasites" infiltrating the country? Either way she'd come prepared. There was no topic she couldn't touch.

Anna flipped on the evening's rerun of The Daily Roundup on rival Avalon News Network. Kirk Sullivan pounded a fist on his desk. The old man was going on another fascist diatribe about government spending and liberal idealogues rotting away traditional values.

Old or not, he looked great under those lights.

~ ~ ~

The ANN building was dull and inconspicuous; nothing but a big concrete slab and bleak, obsidian windows. Outside, a short, slim blonde held the door open as Anna approached.

"Ms. Acevedo!" she said smiling warmly while offering her hand.

Anna shook it and smiled back. "Dakota Ellsworth?"

"Yes," she said. "I'm so glad you made it. Please come in." She was younger than Anna had expected, her rosy face radiating the enthusiasm of a college student at her first internship.

Cold air nipped at Anna's arms as she entered the lobby.

"A bit chilly in here," Anna said.

"Hm? Oh, yes," Ellsworth replied. "Sorry about that. Something wrong with the air conditioning. We're working on it."

Ellsworth led her up an old lift and into her changing room on the tenth floor.

"We'll send someone over to take care of your make-up in just a moment, we're just prepping the set. Mr. Sullivan is so eager to meet you!"

"Thank you so much," Anna said taking a seat in front of the mirror. "I'm looking forward to our discussion."

Ellsworth shut the door softly on her way out. She was perky, enthusiastic. Anna knew the type. She remembered those early days out of college having to work twice as hard as everyone else just to land any network gig she could, even if it meant kissing ass.

Immigrant women like herself were seldom taken seriously in the world of political journalism. They were seen as angry, ill-educated. Exotic eye candy at the most if they fixed themselves up enough.

She balled her hands into fists thinking about it. "This was a mistake," she muttered under her breath. "Sullivan is just going to feed me to the wolves." Anna heard her producer's retort in her head: *Yeah, but wolves are good for ratings.*

Looking up, she caught her tired reflection staring back. The crow's feet along her eyes had begun to carve their way outward like a dry riverbed. The stress of hosting her own show while avoiding murderous zealots was taking its toll on her body, her youth. She smiled. The make-up department had their work cut out for them.

She decided to let her producers know she was getting ready to tape. They'd been ecstatic when she broke the news, told her this was a golden opportunity. She had scoffed. Her show had been hot for a few months. Big deal. The way she saw it she was just a flavor of the month. She needed a ratings spike to keep the momentum going, yes, but doing something like this? But, as always, her producers wanted a little controversy to keep things fresh. She'd learned the hard way that in show business sometimes people needed adversaries, real or imagined, to get things moving. It was too late to back out now.

She unlocked her phone. No reception. *Damn.*

A cold draft blew along her skin, turning her hairs all prickly. She wrapped her arms across her chest and looked around but couldn't find a thermostat in the room. *Why was it so damn cold?* She crossed the room and peered out the door, hoping to spot a handyman or crewmember that could adjust the settings.

Nothing but a cramped, empty hallway. Curious that no one had been shuffling around; every backstage production she'd ever worked on had been a chaotic affair. Before she returned to the changing room, she heard glass breaking in the distance.

"Hello?" she asked aloud. "Is everything okay out there?"

No response.

She shrugged and continued down the hall to check on the noise. It would give her an excuse to scope out the behind-the-scenes action at Avalon.

Anna wound through a maze of dingy, tight corridors, the paint on every wall peeling and flaking like the skin on charred corpses. She came upon a large loading area. Overhead, perched on a catwalk, she saw a smoldering ashtray. Someone had recently been here.

From below, she followed the catwalk's path through a dark, open room littered with crates and folding chairs. A pile of glass had been neatly piled into a dustpan. The sounds of subtle rustling could be heard in the distance. There were voices. Lots of them. Excited, frantic, buzzing. She spotted a long curtain, turned around the bend, and found herself gazing upon the Daily Roundup set. And there under the bright lights sat good ol' boy Kirk Sullivan, waiting patiently as a frenzy of crewmembers powdered his pale, wrinkled face.

Anna thought about introducing herself but decided to let the man get done up first. They were probably waiting for her back at the changing room anyway.

She pivoted to turn back when a small light glimmered in her peripheral vision. On the catwalk just above Sullivan's desk a man unspooled multiple strands of thin fishing wire down to another crewmember who tied the lines around Sullivan's arms, hands and fingers. The man on the rafters pulled on the wire, lifting Sullivan's limbs like a marionette.

Sullivan's chair rolled backwards, revealing a legless torso. Beneath the desk a crewmember stuffed his arm up through a cavity under Sullivan's belly, manipulating his head and jaw like a sock puppet.

Anna stifled a gasp with her hand as her guts twisted themselves into knots. She fought the urge to throw up, pushing down the surge of hot bile in her throat. A flood of tears streamed down her face, dripping off her chin and onto the floor.

"Alright," a tall worker in a red cap said, "hit him with some formaldehyde."

A woman approached Sullivan and jabbed his cheek with a syringe.

"And crank up the A/C!" the tall man said. "His skin is looking a little mushy."

Sullivan whipped his head toward Anna. Her heart skipped a beat.

"Hello, Ms. Acevedo," Sullivan said, his lips not in perfect synchronicity with his words. Or had it been the words of his handler beneath the desk? "Am I pronouncing that right? Ah-say-vay-doh?"

She took a step back the way she came and felt an arm wrap around her waist. Then came the sting of a needle at her neck.

There was only a flicker of lightheadedness before the darkness.

Anna wove in and out of consciousness, surrounded by strange men in the cramped interior of the changing room. She'd been lying on the loveseat from what she could tell.

She struggled to keep her eyelids open as her head pounded. She felt drowsy, weak. Men wearing latex gloves, many of them brandishing saws and scalpels, pinned her arms down. If she hadn't been so drugged, she would have screamed and cried and kicked. As it was, she couldn't move her legs. Her legs!

She craned her neck as far as she could and peered down the length of her body. Her legs were gone. All that remained of her existed just above the waist. Someone slid a bucket under her torso. Her heart began to race and she turned away toward the ceiling, gasping for air like a dying fish.

Dakota Ellsworth stepped into view and caressed Anna's face with cold fingers. "It's best if you don't look," she said in her soft voice.

Anna tried to speak but her throat was dry and scratchy and the only thing her lips could do was quiver.

"Don't worry, you'll look better than ever when we're all done. I promise." Ellsworth gently squeezed Anna's hand.

Anna squeezed back as hard as her muscles would let her. She licked her lips and mouthed, "Why?"

"The experiment was a failure," Ellsworth said, tracing her fingers along Anna's face in small circles. Ellsworth grimaced while pinching her own face, as if feeling some foreign growth. Her skin stretched out as if it were going to snap apart. "Existence is an infirmity. Consciousness, a malady. We realize that now. Life must be turned on itself. But there are so few of us left," she sighed, her eyes scanning the ceiling like someone gazing deeply at the stars. Stars that weren't there. Her words were mad, but Anna saw something in Ellsworth's gaze. Not madness, but startling clarity.

"We sow malice, hate, lies and paranoia until it boils to the surface. Then our viewers do the rest and act out on that hatred. Like good little puppets. You yourself have a built-in viewership that hangs on your every word, frothing at the mouth to act out on a political enemy that threatens their perceived way of life. You'll make an excellent addition to the show."

Ellsworth nodded and another woman approached Anna, quickly applying foundation to her face. Next, Anna felt a slight pressure on her belly and heard the wet, sloshing sounds of things dropping into the bucket. There was no pain before darkness came for her again.

The red light above the camera blinked on and Kirk Sullivan smiled.

"My next guest is the self-appointed Liberal Lioness, Anna Acevedo. Welcome and thank you for joining us on the show tonight."

Through unseen machinations, Anna's head turned toward the camera and at the millions of viewers at home waiting for blood to spill. The lighting captured her flawless complexion and fiery brown eyes perfectly.

She smiled. "It's my pleasure to be here, Kirk."

A Thing with Feathers

Richie Narvaez

My agent grew heavy on my shoulders. With each second, I became dizzier, hazier.

"Tell me again . . ." I said hoarsely, ". . . tell me again about the book deal."

"Of course, darling!" she whispered in my ear, coffee strong on her breath. "Monarch Publishing is offering *you* a $100,000 advance on *The Strangest Sea.* And they want a sequel!"

"But . . . everybody . . . dies . . . at the end."

"Sequels are in! You'll figure it out! They're hungry for it! Hungry, I tell you! And they want you to add more romance and some fantasy elements."

"Wha—?"

"Did I tell you Meryl Estevez will be editing your book? Meryl Estevez!"

"Oh . . . my." My vision blurred. "S'hard . . . to believe."

"Are you not a great writer? Are you not as good as García Márquez? Vargas Llosa?"

"Vargas. . . . My—"

"Is the world not dying to read your words?"

". . . Yeahhhh, I—"

"Then believe it! *Believe* it!" Her tendrils sank deep into my neck, tightened around my spine. "Never lose *hope*."

Her dusty wings fluttered and her full weight settled on me like a battleship, a skyscraper, a moon, and I shivered with bliss.

Hours later, when I left my agent's office, I wanted to celebrate and called my girlfriend, Aracely.

"This is it, baby," I told her. "My moment! The big time. All I hoped for. One hundred grand!"

"I don't know, Edwin. Didn't you just meet this agent? Do you even know if she's legit? She could be a con woman, you know."

"She's not. She knows people. She knows Meryl Estevez."

"Meryl Estevez! She has a jillion Instagram followers."

"See! C'mon, let's get a big steak dinner then get stinking."

"That sounds terrific, Edwin, but I'm afraid Aideliz and I can't. She has her recital tomorrow, remember? I'm getting snacks together now."

I could hear her daughter, Aideliz, in the background rehearsing "This girl is on fiyah!" at the top of her lungs.

"Right. Sorry. I forgot."

I'd met Aracely on Tinder. Her profile had said, "Aquarius," and mine, "Gemini." That was all it took. The vibes were strong, and we averaged a hundred texts a day for a while. I would have moved in with her, but she had her daughter, and I hated wearing clothes in the house, so we put it off. Lately, we'd just been drifting.

"I sent you an invite. The more people in the audience, the better."

"Sure. I wouldn't miss it for the world."

I hung up and called my friend Yoelvis. He was always up for a good time. We agreed to meet at the White Horse Tavern, in the West Village.

I took a stool at the bar and ten minutes later he walked in, in his paunch-filled "Pay No Attention to My Browser History. I'm a Writer!" T-shirt. The first thing he said to me was, "Dude, you look awful."

"Screw you," I said, surprised at how much it sounded like the cackle of a cancerous smoker.

We got a table, and I opened my pleather briefcase to show Yoelvis a bottle of mid-range champagne I'd bought at some point on the way over. Oddly, I couldn't remember where or when.

I said, "Hey, I got a book deal with Monarch Publishing! We're gonna celebrate."

"Wow! Which book?"

"*The Strangest Sea.*"

"Really? That one?"

"Yeah, that one! And they want a sequel. And romance. And a fantasy angle."

"But you despise fantasy and romance. And don't all the characters die at the end?"

Yoelvis was a writer, too, had struggled for years to get his—*yaaaaaawn*—epic spec fic/noir novel accepted. He'd asked me to beta read it, and I tried, I did. But it was twelve hundred pages long. With maps, and a glossary. I couldn't get through it, so I just did a spellcheck and told him it was solid.

The waiter—too good looking to not be a wannabe actor, because: New York—marched over then and chewed gum at my bubbly. "You can't bring in your own liquor. We have champagne here if you want."

"Yeah, no thank you," I said, not wanting to pay fifteen dollars for what was likely a glass of flat liquid. I ordered a Manhattan.

After the waiter left, Yoelvis took out a Swiss Army knife and, under the table, worked open the champagne. When the cork popped, Yoelvis coughed loudly. The waiter gave us a look, but we just twiddled our thumbs.

Whenever his back was turned, Yoelvis and I took turns swigging from the bottle.

"Here's to success!" I said.

"Success!" Yoelvis said. "Hey, I thought you just sent your agent the manuscript last month."

"I did. But this agent loved it! Sent it right out! Monarch, they loved it! Called her to accept it right away! I'm *that* good, you see? I just had to believe in myself!"

Yoelvis was a good friend, but at that moment I could smell his envy, taste it in the air between us like a hot dog burp. I knew what he was going to say next. He toyed with his plastic coaster, like a teenager getting up nerve.

"Hey . . . maybe . . . do you think . . . could you, mmm . . . introduce me to your agent? I haven't had much luck, and if I just had the right agent, I know—"

"I don't think so. Her dance card is full. Sorry, pal," I said.

It wasn't that. I just didn't want to share my agent. I wanted her to focus as much as she could on me. This was *my* chance to rise.

Stumbling home that night, I remembered we'd left the empty champagne bottle under the table. I wished I could've seen that waiter's face when he found it.

Sunday, I went over to Aracely's place in Washington Heights, a pre-WWII building with hallways that smelled of bleach and road-killed skunk. When I came into the apartment, I saw they had hung a banner saying "Congratulations."

Aracely had bought me a six-pack, and she and Aideliz had baked me a cake that said "Author! Author!" The *pastelón* was delish.

With dessert, Aideliz stood on her chair and said, "I hope you become the best, most famous writer in the world!" She sang like it was an aria, in an angelic, clear voice, and took a dramatic bow.

Later, once Aideliz went to sleep, Aracely and I went to her bedroom, got undressed and went at it. In the middle of it, she said, real soft and tender, "Edwin, I want you to know Aideliz and I are very proud of you. We are. We never doubted you."

In response, I released a beer-fart, hoping to show that all was copacetic, hoping to be funny. But it came out louder and ruder-sounding than I intended and after that there was only silence.

I spent my next few days thinking about my book deal. I was on Cloud Nine, Cloud Eleven, hell, Cloud Five Hundred Trillion. My agent had said she would send over the contracts, and I watched my Gmail like it was a kettle.

And I kept watching.

It was taking a long while.

While this waiting was going on, I decided, *What the hell?* I'd go to that Association of American Authors Annual Ball I'd been invited to. Even though I'd been paying my yearly dues, I'd been skipping the monthly AAA meetings, having gotten sick of people bragging about *their* agents, *their* editors, *their* life-changing book deals. But now I finally had something to brag about.

I dressed up, wore my good blazer, not the one from J. Crew.

At the ball, I was happy to enjoy mouthfuls of shrimp cocktail because I'd been feeling kind of wan lately. As I lingered by the food, Ignacia, an acquaintance/rival/one-time-Yaddo-writers-colony-fling, slid next to me, kissed me wetly on the cheek. She wore a thick turtleneck sweater and not enough perfume.

She said, "Hiiii! It's exceptional to see you."

And I said, "Meryl Estevez at Monarch will be editing my novel!"

"*Your* novel. Really?"

Just then a tall woman passing by in a tailored pantsuit 180'd like a Ferrari. I recognized her instantly and began shvitzing.

"Excuse me," Meryl Estevez said. "Did you say my name? Not to be nosy, but I'd love to hear the context."

I shook her hand with gusto. "Holy smokes! Ms. Estevez, it's a pleasure to meet you! Yes, you're going to be editing my novel! I can't tell you how much I'm looking forward to working with you."

"*Et vous êtes qui?*"

Grinning, I told her about the $100,000, two-book deal.

She said, "I have no idea what you're talking about. I know who we read, I know who we sign, and I know I have never heard of you or your book. *Ciao!*" She turned away, searching for someone more interesting, and vroomed back into the crowd.

Ignacia didn't even try to hide her smirk as she moved toward the baked brie. "See you on the best-seller lists!" she said.

I was flabbergasted, embarrassed. I left without having another shrimp.

~ ~ ~

I called my agent as soon as I got outside. No answer. At home, I wrote her a long email. Had I misunderstood what she'd said? Was it another editor at another house, an Erroll Mestevez or something like that!? Should I start on the sequel or what? How much romance should I put in? How much fantasy? And if so, did she think bringing all the *The Strangest Sea* characters back from the dead would be cool, or should I jump ahead a generation? Could I, should I do a prequel? Could she get back to me ASAP?

Days went by.

Weeks.

I didn't want to be *that* author, didn't want to get a rep as a pain to work with, didn't want to screw myself over for any future opportunities. I waited till the end of the following month to send another email.

Nothing.

Months went by.

The euphoria of the book deal waned. I began to wonder about what I wanted. All this uncertainty, all this waiting.

Was all this anxiety worth it?

It was winter before I psyched myself up to see my agent in person. Her office was in an apartment building on the Upper East Side, and the first thing she'd told me when I signed with her was that I should never ever come by without an appointment.

But I needed the lowdown. So all bets were off.

The door guy didn't even look up when I walked past him and took the elevator. When I got off on my agent's floor and to her door, lucky for me another person was just leaving her apartment. Another writer, no doubt, because she wore huge, tinted glasses and a vast scarf that, whatever it had once been made of, was now mostly cat hair.

"A major advance . . ." she wheezed as she stumbled past, hugging the paisley wallpaper, a dreamy grin on her face like she'd just huffed a bag stuffed with lotus leaves, ". . . major."

Inside the apartment/office, my agent was nowhere to be found. I walked into the shag-rugged living room and down the only hallway past a bathroom and to what seemed to be a bedroom.

Spilling out of the bedroom doorway was paper. As I got closer, I realized these were typewritten pages—pages and pages of manuscripts. Closer, I saw the room itself was filled several feet deep by these pages, in a circular pattern with a depression in the middle.

"Edwin! Sunshine!" her voice bellowed from somewhere behind me. Accompanied by the sound of thick, fibrous wings. "How great to see you!" She fluttered down onto my sloping shoulders. "You look gorgeous!"

"Just hold on," I said, trying to twist away. "I—I want to know wha—what's happening with my book deal. I was so stoked. Did I do something wrong?"

She purred, "My dear! Publishing takes time! And patience! This is the Big Four. THE BIG FOUR!"

"I thought it was the Big Five."

"That was last month. Darling, you don't want to be published by some hybrid press run by a loser on a laptop in a garage, would you? Would you?!"

"No, no. Of course not. No."

"Or, worse, darling, you wouldn't want to . . . self-publish?!" She hissed.

"God forbid! No!" I squirmed. "Although it doesn't carry the stigma it once did."

"Don't be a fool! Who else understands you like I do? Who else knows what secret dreams of mainstream acceptance are perched in your soul? Only I do!"

I didn't know anymore. I slumped down, and her tendrils penetrated skin, entered the back of my neck, melded with veins, wrapped themselves around my spine. And sucked.

I surrendered to bliss, the bliss of possibility.

"That's better!" she said, taking a long, noisy slurp. "Now! Let me tell you about this movie option I just got for you. Big time! Jackpot! Spielberg himself is interested, and, mmmmmmm, his people have . . . wait. Wait! Something's wrong. I can taste it." She removed herself from me, leaving me feeling like a gaping wound.

"You. Have. Doubts." She spat. "Bitter doubts."

"What? Me? No! *No?* Maybe."

"Do you want a book deal or not?"

"I think so."

"Think so? You've got no—" she flapped her long, thin, hollow tongue against her lips—"no *hope*. I can't work with that."

"It'll come back. Promise."

"If you want me to keep working for you, dear, you'll have to do better than that."

"What do you mean? What do you want me to do?"

The next day Yoelvis met me at the White Horse Tavern. When I walked in he was already there, his smile wide as a keyboard. He wore a T-shirt that read "I Believe in Truth, Beauty, and the Oxford Comma."

"I'm so glad, you called me. *So* glad," he said, his voice kind of hoarse.

"Yeah, I'm sure you are."

"I was going to call you, in fact!" he said, then coughed loudly.

I said, "I wanted to talk to you about my a—"

"That's just it. I have great news! I signed a deal! Got an agent! This guy in midtown. He knows all the right people. Got me a deal at Emperor Books."

"Emperor?"

"Yeah, man. You know I've been trying for years. Rejection after rejection. I got a folderful. All I've ever needed was just one agent to believe in me!"

"Sure, sure," I said. "Congratulations! Cheers and everything."

That waiter from the last time we were both there came around. He must've recognized us because he gave us a stink eye that would've earned the Academy Award for Stink Eyes.

As he was ordering, Yoelvis had a coughing fit and bent over. I noticed dark red scars on the back of his neck. I knew those scars well. I'd seen them in the mirror.

That weekend I went to Aracely's apartment, depressed as a union representative. On top of that, since it wasn't a special occasion, dinner would be frozen pizza.

"Sorry about the pizza," Aracely said, tossing it into the oven with a crack. "This was the only thing in the fridge. But it won't always be like this. Good times are ahead. I know that in my heart."

Sweet Aracely. So full of hope. . . .

That made me stop, made me think. *Such hope.*

Could it work? Would my agent accept . . . ?

"Aracely," I said, "I was wondering . . ."

"Yeah?"

At that very second, tumbling out of the bedroom came Aideliz, doing a cartwheel while yelling, "Since you been gone!"

I stopped and thought again. *Of course.* Look at her with her face, her big, bright eyes. She was a fountain—a goddamn *factory*—of hope. She had the corner market on hope. She was a worldwide conglomerate of hope.

"Aideliz, honey," I said. "How would you like to come meet my agent?"

"Okay," she said, innocent as a pup.

"Edwin, what are you talking about?" Aracely said. "Why would she want to meet your agent?"

"Uh, she might want to be a writer someday. She has aspirations."

"She wants to be a singer. She has talent."

"But younger writers are in demand. They're photogenic, social media savvy. Publishers love that. They're like an investment."

"I don't like the sound of that."

"She could do a middle grade memoir."

"A memoir? She's ten, and the worst thing that has happened to her was my not letting her dye her hair blue."

"It won't take long. It'll be a fun ride. On the subway, of course."

"Yay, a ride!" Aideliz said.

Aracely poured me some wine and then water on top of it, to stretch it. Looking at me, she said, "Aideliz, did you wash your hands yet today?"

The kid shook her head. "Not since Thursday."

"Go wash your hands."

Aideliz somersaulted to the bathroom. Aracely and I sat in silence waiting for my cardboard slices. When the kid came out, I went to the john.

It was after I came back that I heard a hacking cough. The kid. Then I saw: the back of Aideliz's neck. Dark red scars.

Aracely caught my look.

"No! No, you don't. Don't you dare judge," she said. "I have dreams, too. I have ambitions. I don't want to stay in this stinking apartment forever. And Aideliz has talent! There was a talent scout outside the school yesterday. He explained everything. He says she's a shoo-in for *America's Got Talent.* This could be her moment."

"Sure," I repeated. "Her moment."

I stuck around for the pizza—because: why not?—and then I left.

⁂

I stomped around the city afterward, to move, to not think, from the Upper West Side down to the Village.

I found myself back at the White Horse, got the same snotty wannabe actor waiter again. I ordered a Manhattan and let it get warm in my hand. What was I going to do? My literary career looked stalled in place, and, to be honest, I wasn't even sure I wanted it to go anywhere.

When I went to pay the check, I dropped my credit card. The waiter bent down to get it and there it was. I should've known. Dark red scars.

Once you start looking for something, you find it. On the street. On the subway. In bars, franchise restaurants, bodegas. Port Authority not so much, but they'd be getting theirs soon.

So many scars. So many dreamers.

I didn't go home. I sat on a bench outside Central Park and watched the sky grow lighter. I made my way to my agent's.

The door was ajar. I ripped it open, and filling the doorway were books, stacks and stacks of books, some going as high as the ceiling. A narrow gap between the teetering piles formed a corridor that led me to the back room.

My agent lay in her nest, now ringed with books and boxes of more books. She was bloated, enormous.

"Edwin! Darling!"

"Are you okay?"

"My dear." She rolled herself over to the bottom of a staired stack and began to climb it. She motioned for me to move toward its summit.

"I . . . don't know."

"But, darling, I have seen the future, and yours will be lit up by five-star reviews!"

"Did Monarch—"

"Who needs Monarch? I'm starting my own publishing company! You sign a contributory contract and your book will be out in less than a week! And what's more, you'll make forty percent of the profits. On ebooks, that is."

"Didn't you say small publishing companies were a bad thing?"

"I was so, so wrong! It's a much steadier . . . vein. And consider this, darling: We can publish your book as is. No added romance or fantasy. In fact, not even a single edit."

"Well, I'd like a copy edit."

"That's what spellcheck is for! And you can even design your own cover."

Her wings, gleaming now, fluttered slowly, causing a breeze and pushing the dust in the apartment in my face.

I sneezed, sniffled. "I guess."

"Don't be abashed, Edwin. Turn around."

I did as I was told.

"Ahhhh," she said, smacking her lips, "there's absolutely nothing in this world like fresh hope."

Night Shifts

Toni Margarita Plummer

The pimp's name would have to be Jorge. Not that he was really a pimp. He only aspired to be one, though he would never admit this. I knew better, of course. He fancied all of us his potential whores. All except for me, that is. But then he had found another use for me: the madam, the mother hen. They'll listen to you, he said, it will sound better coming from you. And I got a little something extra for this service, so I didn't complain.

At the start of most nights, Jorge ambles over to me, already sweating, his stomach straining against his belt. He's a big man. More of him to love, some might say. More of him to something, that's for sure.

Tonight another young woman trails behind him. I have to hand it to him, he never fails to catch them. Keeping them is another story, and that's where I come in. "I've got a new girl for you," he tells me. "Help her out, yeah, Lorene?" He smiles politely at the woman, even bowing slightly, and stalks back to his office to count money.

The woman stands uncertainly, holding the crook of her elbow with one hand. Then, as if she's made up her mind about something, she leans forward and extends her hand. "I'm Ana." They don't usually want to shake my hand and this amuses me. I give mine, covered in black lace. I've taken to wearing gloves, and it's become a trademark of mine. It just got tiring, the men noticing how cold my hands are and making a show of trying to warm them. As if they ever could. Once that chill gets in, there's nothing anyone can do.

"Lorene," I introduce myself.

I never use my real name for jobs like this. For one, everyone would mangle it, and I've been mangled enough. I chose the name Lorene because of the character in *From Here to Eternity*. This is a dance hall, or gentleman's club, like the one in the movie where Lorene worked. Jorge really tries to sell the "gentleman" part too. And wants me to sell it. This is a decent place, he says. No nudity or undressing of any kind. No heavy groping, though light petting and close dancing are permissible. I don't mind that there's no alcohol like some do. The drink I crave is not something sold at a bar, although it's as easily obtained, I suppose. I just need to puncture the surface, like pulling the tab on a can. I do wish I could smoke though. I would blow smoke rings, like one of the women in the old movies I like to watch.

Unfortunately, this isn't a movie.

And in the novel it wasn't a dance hall. It was a whorehouse. Lorene was a whore.

I pat the space beside me and Ana lowers herself onto the plush, tiger-striped sofa that is a shade of pink I hope does not exist in nature. She squints under the rosy lights beaming down on us. She is still coming to terms with who she is now. She is one of us, and we are all items on display. There is no salesman or pitch. Well-packaged, we'll sell ourselves.

The rest of the women sit in two rows of chairs. We are situated so that we face the bar and tables where the men sit across the room. We are to wait here, ready, while they deliberate over who they will choose first.

One will want to try the new girl. Though Ana is nothing special, I can tell that right away. She looks like most of the other women here, with that same mix of features. The dark hair, the lighter skin. I am surrounded by the children of the conquerors and have been for some time. Her dress is all wrong though. Too modest and too long, like she's out on a first date at a nice, moderately priced restaurant.

"Waitress or cashier?" I ask her. Lacking a cigarette, I compensate by taking out a compact mirror and powdering my nose. I know I really shouldn't bring out the mirror, but the people in this place never notice anything.

"Excuse me?"

"The position you originally applied for. Waitress or cashier?"

Ana blinks. "Bookkeeper."

"Bookeeper. That's a new one. Jorge's getting fancy."

Most of these women are confused by the way I talk, but Ana smiles. "How long have you been working here?"

"Too long and not long enough."

The men continue to nurse their non-alcoholic beer. Even though they don't need to come up with a line or any pretense, they won't approach us for a while. It's always like this at the beginning of the night. Some of the women sigh or tap their feet in impatience. If you are like me, you know how to wait. If you wait, the insect will wander into the web, eventually. I take this time to launch into my spiel.

"When you first go in, ask them if they've been here before. Make sure they know how much they're supposed to tip you. Don't let them rip you off. And try not to stay in there for over an hour." I look down at her bare wrist, note her veins. "Next time wear a watch. Say you gotta take a break. You don't want them just tipping you for one hour when you've been in there with them for two. They'll do that."

Ana nods. She's trying. She's trying to show interest, to give this a shot. But I can tell the drive just isn't there. She watches the men in business suits who are engrossed in the baseball game.

"Never mix women and sports," she jokes, rather lamely.

I smirk.

Some of the women dig through little purses. No cell phones are allowed, and if the guy manning the cash table sees the light of one, he'll confiscate it. It wouldn't look right, Jorge says. It wouldn't look right if it seemed these women had a life outside this building. I don't, of course, but I am not most women.

Ana glances around, as if to see if anyone is watching. "Do you want to see something?"

Before I can decline, she removes a folded paper from under her bra strap. It's a print-out from one of those websites that tells you the make-up of your ancestry. Twenty percent of this, forty percent that. Ridiculous. I heard they use a sample of saliva in order to tell. Saliva disgusts me. You would think they'd need someone's blood for something like this. Blood is the only thing that can tell you someone's story.

"I found a new ancestor of mine. My family goes back far in Los Angeles. Really, really far." She says this with pride, and without a hint of the sorrow still buried in me.

"I did this for my daughter. I want her to know where her family comes from. Do you have any children?"

"I had a daughter once."

"Once?" she asks gently, carefully.

"All grown up and gone."

"But you look so young."

I just smile.

More men come in and sit down. A few are starting to select women and take them into the dance room. That's where we should all want to go. The man takes you in there, dances with you, maybe sits on a couch with you and orders a few drinks. There are TV's. It costs him thirty dollars an hour in there with you. And when it's done, he tips you. The tip should match the bill, I tell Ana.

She is still looking over her print-out when she's waved in.

"Go get 'em," I tell her.

Soon after, I'm called in by a man I've seen before. At least I think so. When you've worked as many nights as I have, they all blend together. The men especially.

My repeat customers are different from those of the other women. They don't come for smiles or feigned laughter. They come for my direct looks. I see them and I don't flinch. I don't shy away. There is nothing about them I fear. Nothing that shocks me. Why would it?

The new ones, they choose me for my darkness, my face. Where are you from, they ask, and I always tell them the truth. I am from here. But I don't belong here anymore.

Some of the new ones come talking, looking for sympathy, and these are the ones I find hardest to deal with. These are the ones who for some reason think that the woman whose company they are paying for is possibly their soulmate. It's the male fantasy of the whore with the heart of gold: a mythical creature who has been fucked every which way by every kind of foul asshole but somehow is still sweet and kind and trusting, who can still fall in love. Every whore I've ever known would just as soon cut your throat. And I've never blamed them. Some throats are begging for it.

I see Ana on the dance floor with her customer. He has both hands on her waist and they are slowly rotating in awkward shuffles of their feet. She moves stiffly, but when she see me she smiles over the man's shoulder.

My next customer sees no need to put up the pretense of dancing and only rhythmically rubs his crotch against my dress. I've no feeling there, not for what's in his pants anyways. His neck is close to me though, and I allow myself a look, a whiff. But I have a rule; I don't shit where I work. I've made that mistake before and I have a good gig here. I can pay for my no-frills basement apartment in cash. No need to complicate things.

My next customer is an elderly man who loves to tango, and dip. When the song ends, he sticks a bill into my cleavage.

I go outside and Ana is sitting in one of the rows, her legs crossed primly.

It is at *this* time of the night that I start to get impatient. I am itching to be out on the street, to grab a bite to eat. But Jorge insists we wait until midnight, no matter how slow things get. A blond woman returns from the bar with a steaming cup of noodles, and I try not to crinkle my nose at the smell. If I have to wait to eat, why can't everyone else?

Finally it is midnight. I find Ana in the locker room and tap her on the shoulder. Jorge will want to see her.

"How did it go?" he asks, sitting at his desk while we stand in front of the doorway.

"Fine, fine," Ana says. "But, I don't think I'll be coming back."

"What?" Jorge looks up. "But you just started. Look at Lorene. She's making two hundred dollars a night. You stick around, you could make a lot of money here. Tell her, Lorene."

Jorge has to learn, some things you can't force. "It sounds like she's made up her mind," I say.

"Is this what I pay you for?" He slams his fist on the desk.

I cross my arms over my chest and lean in the doorway. He knows he can't scare me, but that doesn't stop him from trying.

Ana clears her throat. "You said I'd get 10% of the bill?"

"For one night's work? That's only for steady girls. You trying to bleed me? You made your tips!"

Ana blanches, the blood draining from her face. I can hear her heart thumping from where I stand. She casts me a glance and leaves.

Jorge glares at me, and I smile, showing my teeth. "Why so upset, boss? Girls like her are a dime a dozen."

"What do you know about it, puta?" he spits.

The smile doesn't leave my face. He hates that, I know.

Outside I see Ana walking to her car in the reserved lot under the 10-freeway. She takes out her keys and the others emerge from the shadows to surround her.

The others don't usually come here, but I poached last night. It was a tasty treat, one I didn't want to deny myself. Now these others are here for their share.

I should leave them to it. These girls are a dime a dozen, after all.

So I'm not entirely sure why I make my way over, gingerly avoiding the metro tracks. The others stop their encroachment and Ana looks up to see me. Even from this distance I can see the fright in her eyes.

I stop in front of them and put my hands on my hips. "Sweet of you all to come by to see me! What you in the mood for? Want to hit the clubs?"

"You were on Figueroa last night," the leader of the pack says, no pleasantries.

I give them all a good once-over. It would probably be a fair match. Their four to my one.

"So I was."

They wait, staring me down and eyeing Ana. Just then Jorge steps out of the building and walks toward us, to his car in the lot. He gives us a hateful glance and mutters something about loitering. He really is an asshole, it's a wonder he's lived this long.

I lock eyes with the leader and incline my head ever so slightly, toward my dear boss. Their attention shifts.

"Jorge, I don't think you've met my friends," I say in my sweetest voice.

"I have no desire to meet your friends," he says, searching his bag. He doesn't even notice the danger until he's cornered. "Lorene," he says. That's all.

Ana scrambles into her car and starts the engine.

"Help them out, yeah, Jorge?" I turn away, waving my hand in the air. His scream pierces the night, deliciously.

I was right. It did sound better coming from him.

Between Going and Staying

Lilliam Rivera

For this funeral service, Dolores selects The Selena™ kit and pairs it with sky-high stilettos. The kit comes with a thin silicone prosthetic bodysuit that covers her slender frame and a real-time, face-tracking and internal-projection video mask to map the face of a twenty-year-old Latina over her own. Unlike the ridiculous rubber suits worn by other weepers, her kit is top of the line. This is the fourth funeral Dolores has worked this week, the second to be held in the Valley of the Tears Funeral Stadium.

"Again," Dolores says to the Codigo5G. She greases her body with a special glue to provide suction and listens to the machine recite the bio once more:

Client: José Antonio Ramírez de la Guarda.
Born in Sinaloa, Mexico
Discovered singing at his cousin's quinceañera party
Lead vocalist of the narcocorrido band The Super Capos
Went solo with the single "When I See You I'll Kill You"
Death listed as cardiovascular
Doliente Order: The Selena™

Location: Valley of the Tears Funeral Stadium
Fee: $35,990.33 dollars
Transport provided, arriving in thirty minutes and counting.

"Cardiovascular? Yeah, right," Dolores says to herself. She heard the real story on the deceased singer from her driver—the accordion player from his former group The Super Capos took him down. Such is the life. Dolores almost fired the driver for telling her. He knows now never to speak to her of such things.

Although transactions have long been handled virtually, most people still follow the old tradition of submitting payments in odd-numbered denominations to ward off bad luck. Dolores doesn't really care. She just wants the money deposited way in advance of the service.

"New search. Gold beds, the most expensive brands," she says. The Codigo5G displays a multitude of options for her. Long gold beds float around her dressing room. With this payment, Dolores plans to replace her current silver furniture with this season's gold. The walls of her high-rise apartment already radiate the gilded hue, as does the large vanity table she now faces. She's glancing at the floating beds, envisioning which would match perfectly against her olive skin, when the Codigo's search is interrupted.

"*New Message.*"

Dolores sighs. There's a backlog of requests for her. To be a Doliente is to serve the living and the dead, her mother once said. Dolores was ten years old when she first saw her mother work as a Doliente. Back then there were no high-tech skins or tacky rubber suits to choose from. Instead, her mother dressed like a little girl with a long black wig and a child's puffy floral dress. Dolores thought she looked ridiculous.

"Continue," Dolores says.

"*Doliente order request from Señora Raya: M'ija, come home. Your community needs you.*"

"Mom, I can't. I'm fully booked," Dolores says in a huff. "Relay message, Codigo."

Why does her mother insist on bothering her with trivial funeral services? Dolores stopped booking charity appearances long ago. It was her idea to add a bit of glamour to being a Doliente. Singing, choreography. In a short time, Dolores went from bookings at funerals held in small, forgotten towns to televised tributes.

No other Doliente comes close to her popularity. Her mother doesn't get that she's on a whole other level.

"*Response: It's important. M'ija, come home.*"

Dolores adjusts the skin and checks the time. The car service will pick her up soon. She hasn't seen her mom in close to a year although she schedules a video chat every two weeks. That should be more than enough.

"Codigo, relay this message: Who is the client and which Doliente do they want to order? And I'm not saying I'm going to do it."

Silence follows.

"*Response: She wants the Pascola and the service will be held en el pueblo. En La Cruz. It's for The Disappeared, Dolores.*"

She immediately glances over to the Pascola mask that hangs above her silver bed. The mask is crudely made from painted wood with long strands of goat hair poking out around its frame. This particular mask was a gift from Melody, her lover from a long time ago.

"Did Melody put you up to this?" Dolores asks. "She should know better than to use you as some sort of messenger."

"*Response: I can't speak about this with you over the Codigo. It's too delicate an issue. Let me come over and explain the situation in person.*"

"No, that's not happening. I don't have time," Dolores says.

"*Response: You must make time. Don't be so hardheaded. Have you forgotten your own people? Too busy tending to strangers instead of those who truly matter? You are a Doliente. You serve the community, not some rich people from the city.*"

Dolores refuses the guilt her mother tries to pass on to her. She paid her dues like everyone else who left La Cruz. When did it fall on Dolores to carry the burden of a whole town?

"*Response: It's about Melody. Please don't make me say this over the Codigo. Get on video and let me see your face at least. I don't ask for much in my old age—*"

"Fine!"

Her video mask defaults to neutral: the expressionless, almost bored face of a young Latina. She won't bother to turn the mask on since Dolores plans to grant her mother only five minutes of video time. No more.

It takes a few seconds for the video to transmit. Her mother's eyes are rimmed red as if she's been crying. To see her in such a state makes Dolores nervous. She braces herself for the ask because she already knows that it will involve more than she is capable of giving.

"So what does Melody want? And be quick, Mom, my transport is arriving," she says with bite. "Does she want money to fund some school? Just tell me how much."

"*M'ija*. This is not just another job. *Ay*, I wish you weren't in that skin." Her mother's voice has an edge to it, too. "It happened a little under a week ago. Men came heavily armed. These so-called men covered their faces with masks. Thirteen were taken away, mostly students from the university."

Dolores ignores the increased rate of her heart. She understands what it means to be taken away. No one is ever returned. The unrest is nothing new to La Cruz. Yet, to see her mother affected by it so strongly is distressing.

"Melody asked you to perform la Pascola," her mother continues. The redness on her face grows. "It was written in a notebook hidden in her aunt's house. Just in case."

"In case of what?" Dolores says. Anxiety reaches its peak. "What are you talking about?"

Tears roll down her mother's cheeks.

"Melody wrote that if anything happened to her, she would want la Pascola. That only you could do the dance. I'm so sorry." She pauses, unable to continue. Her face appears distorted, unkempt from such heavy emotions. "Melody is one of The Disappeared. They took her that night with her students."

Dolores searches her mother's crumbled face. Waits for her to say it's a mistake, for the words to form meaning. She tries to fall deeper into her Selena™ skin, to press her thin body against the prosthetic flesh.

"Dolores? Did you hear me?"

Everything sounds muffled, as if Dolores is being immersed in a pool of water. Her thoughts reel back to Melody and the arguments they used to have, of her begging Melody to move with her to the city. The threats were real even back then. Melody refused to give in. "We are La Cruz, and no one will run me out of my own home," she would say. What happened the night Melody was taken? What did they do to her? To the thirteen? Dolores's room tilts slightly to the left.

"*M'ija*, are you alright?" her mother asks. "I can't tell with that *maldita* skin on! Answer me. Please."

"Yes." Dolores barely whispers the word. "Yes. I heard you. I have to go."

She cuts the transmission, leaving the image of her mother frozen on the screen.

Melody. It can't be. Dolores refuses to accept the news. She is unable to process it.

"*Transport arriving in ten minutes.*"

The sound of the Codigo startles her. She doesn't know how long she's sat there staring at her mother's grieving face. Dolores gathers her stuff and prepares to meet her driver. Her bones feel like they will break. She can hide inside this skin. That is what she intends to do.

"Codigo, repeat the bio."

The Pascola mask appears to follow her movements.

Dolores steps out of the car and the throngs of people reach for her, yelling her current Doliente name—"Selena! Selena!"—while thrusting large bouquets of *cempasúchil* at her. Some are real flowers, bright and yellow. Some are made of paper. Her video mask grins back at them as she selects a couple of the bouquets.

Thoughts of Melody plague her. It's impossible to banish them no matter how hard she tries to concentrate on the task ahead of her. How Melody had freckles across the bridge of her nose. How she fed some feral cat and called it Chente after the singer even though she was allergic to the animal. How Melody pulled Dolores's hair while she kissed her neck.

"This way, Miss Selena. Don't worry, I'll take care of you." A burly security guard with a manicured beard recognizes her and pushes the crowd aside so she can enter the stadium. The need to lean into him is immediate. Her skin's hand appears steady. Yet, inside she is torn up. The guard leads her away from the aggressive crowd and down a long hallway.

"I'm a huge fan," he says. "I saw you last month at The Glory Is Yours Stadium. That Octavio Paz poem you recited gave me goose bumps and—"

Dolores gently squeezes his arm. She draws nearer to him and quietly recites the words to "Hermandad"—"Soy hombre: duro poco y es enorme la noche. Pero miro hacia arriba: las estrellas escriben. . . ."

Although the poem is short she still waits to make sure that the guard follows every word. Remembering the poem is easy. She has an arsenal of memorized pieces always at the ready. Dolores is also aware that the security guard will no doubt share this moment with the media. She has cultivated such moments many times before.

The guard's eyes well up and in that instant, Dolores catches an image of a nineteen-year-old Melody standing right beside him. Melody's dark, wavy hair sways in some unknown breeze and she's wearing an oversized man's shirt, the one with the slight tear on the collar. Her delicate hands hold her worn copy of *Octavio Paz: Collected Poems*. Her former lover stands there as real as the gun that hangs from the security guard's belt. Melody stares at Dolores with a familiar look of judgment.

How can it be? Dolores clutches the security guard's arm. How can Melody be here? So close that Dolores can simply reach out to touch her cheek. So close that she can smell her perfume, the tiny bit of vanity Melody allowed herself. Dolores' fingers dig deeper into the guard's arm.

When Melody opens her mouth to speak, Dolores begins to shake uncontrollably.

"What are you doing here?" Dolores cries out.

"Sorry?" the guard asks. "Is everything alright, Miss Selena?"

And just like that, Melody vanishes.

"Umm. Oh, it's nothing," Dolores says. Her video mask displays a slight smile. Behind the mask Dolores is frightened. The security guard, embarrassed by his own emotions, silently walks her to the stage.

It must be guilt, Dolores thinks. Guilt has her seeing a young Melody. She follows the guard and tries to bury the increasing dread.

When Dolores decided to move to the big city to expand her Doliente services, Melody accused her of selling out. Melody always said that Dolores was blessed with a gift for those who suffered, not for those who caused the suffering. Melody would never have approved of her latest gig reassuring the Ramírez family, a family known for their ties to the cartel. What had Melody said to her once? "We all have blood on our hands, however we have the ability to stop the bleeding." Back then, Dolores believed her. Or maybe she just wanted to be with her. It was a stupid time.

Dolores is given the signal to begin. She steps into the limelight and the audience goes quiet.

"*Noche de ronda. Que triste pasa, que triste cruza por mi balcón.*" Dolores sings the first verse of the song "Noche De Ronda" by Agustín Lara. Each word falls like a hammer. The tune must travel far across the stadium to the very top bleachers, and not just in volume—they must feel it, too. It's not hard to do. The song brings her right back to memories of La Cruz when Melody listened to scratchy recordings while they planned their future together. A future that will never happen.

"*Mi corazón se rompe.*" This last verse is not part of the song. It is her own addition. She repeats it three times: my heart breaks. The audience stands and claps thunderously, throwing flowers onto the stage. Inside her false skin, Dolores tries to maintain her composure. The hurt is present right beside her on that vast stage.

"We are here today to remember a man whose gift for song came from the gods," Dolores says. "With this very gift he has touched every single one of us."

Dolores turns and faces the body of the deceased José Ramírez, which is on display inside a glass box elevated above the stage. The dead singer is seated on a stool wearing his infamous fringed leather jacket and holding a guitar.

"I cannot claim to have had the good fortune to know José." Dolores bows her head regretfully. Then she faces the Ramírez family, who are seated on a balcony behind bulletproof glass. The mother appears stoic, dressed in white; Ramírez's wife, sitting next to her, cries hysterically. "He was like our brother, our cousin, our father. A man who could make our hearts soar in one instant and bring us down to our knees in prayer the next, simply with his words."

She kneels down and accepts a bouquet of *cempasúchil* from a teenage girl who has her hair styled just like The Selena™.

"Maybe you are too young to remember this song. Those who do will never forget it, or the first time José shared his talent to the world."

Dolores sings a simple children's song about candy. In mid-verse, her voice cracks. Josés mother cries.

"Why did José leave us?" Dolores beats her chest with the flowers, scattering yellow petals on the stage. The emotions are real. There is no way to exorcise her feelings for Melody through what she is being paid to do onstage each night. "There were still more songs for him to bring us. Still more smiles left."

The audience yells out in agreement. The women raise their hands, shouting José's name. The men hold their fists up.

A sea of yellow cowboy hats—his favorite headgear—fills the stadium.

"I can't continue. Can you?" Dolores asks the audience. "Who here has the courage I need to continue? Who?"

Men hold out glasses of liquor for her. The next gesture is one she's done hundreds of times before. The audience expects her to share a drink with them. When Dolores bends to accept the shot of Damiana from a young man in a yellow cowboy hat, she's rendered speechless. Next to him stands Melody. Dolores knows it's not really her, that her mind must be playing tricks. Still, Dolores falters.

Melody's lips are bare. She never wore make-up, didn't need to. This is the Melody she met when she first started college. When Dolores walked up to her to ask her for directions to the cafeteria and all Dolores could think about was how beautiful her full lips were. Melody holds up a drink for Dolores. She stares deep into Dolores' eyes, imploring her to take the glass.

"No. No. No," Dolores wails. She drops to the floor and covers her face with her hands to shield herself. "Why are you haunting me?"

For a long moment, Dolores forgets where she is and what she is supposed to do next.

The audience doesn't notice this hiccup. They think it's part of the service and shout words of encouragement at her to continue. Dolores is inconsolable. When a stage handler comes over to make sure she is okay, only then does Dolores dare to open her eyes. When she does, Melody is gone.

The stage handler helps her stand. José Ramírez's mother lifts her glass of liquor and toasts the weeper. She must go on.

"To. . . . To. . . ." Dolores stumbles over her words. "To José." She drinks a shot of Damiana offered to her.

The performance continues without any further interruptions.

~ ~ ~

The security guard from earlier is waiting to escort her back to her car. He goes on about the service. Inside her skin, Dolores' naked body is drenched with sweat and tears. She is worried that The Selena™ will slide off of her and reveal her true self. It's not possible, the technology behind the kits is so advanced.

"Are you ready?" asks the guard.

She braces herself for the crowd. There will be no moments with her fans tonight. She wants to go home to peel off this body. To get away from these hallucinations and retreat into her secluded high-rise where she feels safe and protected among her silver belongings. The past will not engulf her present.

A group of young people crowd around her as soon as she steps outside. At first, Dolores mistakes them for fans. She soon catches their angry expressions. They hold up signs: JUSTICE FOR LA CRUZ 13! WE ARE ALL THE DISAPPEARED! WE DEMAND JUSTICE!

"Doliente, what do you have to say about this?" a teenage boy yells at her. "Stop hiding behind your kits. Stop working for murderers. Justice for La Cruz Thirteen!"

Another girl grabs her skin's arm. The girl's face is splattered with red dye, a mask of fake blood.

"What are you doing to stop the violence?" the girl screams. Dolores tries to pull away. The girl has a firm grip.

"Let me go," Dolores says.

"You are one of us," the girl says. "Step out of your kit."

The security guard pushes the protester away. After a bit of jostling, Dolores jumps into her waiting car. The driver tries to move forward. The protesters block the exit.

"Justice for The Disappeared! Justice for La Cruz Thirteen!"

"They're directing us to the other side of the stadium," the driver says. "Just sit back. I'll have you out of here in no time."

Dolores can't look away from their anger. Melody was once like them. Melody believed that change can be demanded. That voices will be heard if they were willing to shout loud enough. That's not true, is it? You need money to have any kind of power. No one will listen to poor people from some insignificant town.

Something hits the car window. There's no fear of the window shattering, however the jolt is real all the same. The driver cuts a quick turn and drives away from the commotion.

Dolores tries to calm down, to take deep breaths. Her skin has an imprint of a red hand. The tragedy from La Cruz stands before her tonight. She can't look away anymore. There is nowhere for her to hide.

"Codigo, search La Cruz and cross-check with The Disappeared," Dolores says.

"*On January first, a small group of students from the University of La Cruz staged a protest against the school's ties with drug cartels. The agitators accused the university of accepting monies hidden under the guise of educational donations. The next day, eleven students and their two academic advisors disappeared from the campus. Authorities have been unable to locate their whereabouts.*"

Agitators. Even the press is unwilling to upset the cartels. The Codigo shares more articles that say the same thing. Most don't even bother to list the names of the people taken away, as if they never really existed. Nothing more than trouble-makers upsetting the order of things.

Dolores never questions who pays for her Doliente gigs. The larger the payment, the greater the likelihood it's from someone tied to the cartels. Who doesn't have ties to them in some way? From the manicurist to the waiter serving food in some small diner, they are all connected. Dolores plays only a small role. She is their weeper for hire. She picks and choses when she works. Dolores is not beholden to the cartels. How long has she been telling herself this? There is no one around to hold her accountable except her mother.

"Codigo, relay this message to Miss Raya: Mom, I can list many other Dolientes who will give a touching service for half the pay."

"*Response: No, Dolores. You can't do that.*"

"Why me? I haven't seen Melody in years," Dolores sobs. "I have nothing to offer. Nothing real."

"*Response: Dolores, this is not about you. Remember what I taught you. A Doliente's role is to bring comfort to those suffering. In return, you are comforted.*"

"How can you be so sure?" Dolores says. "I can't do this."

"*Response: Come to La Cruz tomorrow. You must.*"

Her mother ends the transmission first.

The driver drops her off and Dolores heads straight to her dressing room where she stores her collection of Doliente kits. The Lupe™ is the skin of an old lady, hunched over with long, gray hair and a cane. The Vicente™ is the skin of a ranchero; The Rocío™, a kit of a little girl. Dolores ignores the technically advanced kits designed to convey sadness and walks further into the dressing room.

Dolores presses a button to display the Pascola costume. The Pascola includes a long, white linen top that hangs over matching pants. A thick leather belt with metallic bells goes around the waist, into which the large wooden rattle is tucked. Strings of giant silk moth cocoons filled with fine stones are wrapped around each of the weeper's legs.

Underneath those items is a small wooden mask. Unlike the other Doliente kits, this mask will not conceal the face. The weeper who performs the Pascola must dance with the mask on the back of their head. The mask is said to represent a wild mountain spirit. For Dolores it means the inability to hide and that scares her more than anything else. She lives her life hidden behind her kits.

Dolores peels off The Selena™ video mask and skin. She stands before her mirror naked, a thin woman with an almost boyish figure. Small hips and breasts. Cropped black hair. A body made to wear skins. Melody loved this body once. The day Dolores left La Cruz was the day she left pleasure and love behind.

Now Melody is gone forever and the woman that stands before her in the mirror seems unrecognizable.

The driver veers to the left, away from the glistening city. The landscape soon shifts from bold, slick lines in vibrant colors to dull, disheveled buildings in disrepair. Dolores cradles the wooden Pascola mask on her lap and debates whether to instruct the driver to turn around and go back. With every bump, the bells on the hems of her pant-legs and sleeves ring.

"Music, please," says Dolores.

The car automatically turns the stereo system on and the first song that plays is "*Hasta que te conocí*" by Juan Gabriel.

"*No sabía, de tristezas, ni de lágrimas. . . .*" The singer sings of once being happy before he met the one love that broke his heart.

"Turn off," she says. How the world conspires to mock her.

There are bags under her eyes from lack of sleep. Dolores practiced the Pascola dance throughout the night even though the steps came back to her as soon as she put on the costume. The last time she danced the Pascola was at a rally that Melody had orchestrated. One of her favorite professors had been fired. On that occasion, the dance was symbolic, mourning how the university was killing the students' creativity. By then, Dolores had already made the decision to leave. After the performance, they lay beside each other in silence with Dolores' chin resting against Melody's bare back. Neither of them said it but Dolores knew it was over.

The driver reaches the entrance of La Cruz and Dolores' anxiety increases. A dread envelops her. Will Melody appear to her here as she had at the Valley of the Tears Stadium? Her former lover has summoned her back to the place she vowed never to return to. Yes, it was her mother's doing, but there is something more powerful bringing her here, too. This scares her. To be seen by Melody like this without a skin. Vulnerable. She foolishly searches for signs of her only love as they pass familiar streets. Is she losing her mind? Dolores holds tight to the mask.

"We're almost there, Miss." The driver turns onto a dusty road. The address she gave him was her mother's house. From there her mother had promised to direct them to the performance area. The driver pulls up to the house and Dolores instructs him to honk the horn. Within minutes, Dolores' mother comes out in a black dress. Her long, white hair flows past her shoulders. She's aged even more since the last time they saw each other.

"Welcome home, *m'ija*," her mother says, entering the car. They exchange an uncomfortable hug. The lenses of her glasses are thick, proof of her refusal to get eye surgery even though Dolores has offered to pay for everything.

"You look thinner," Dolores says.

Her mother hushes away the comment with a white lace handkerchief she holds in her hand.

"You look thin, too," she responds. "Do you eat at all? And this hair?"

Her mother tugs at a short strand. Dolores gently pushes her mother's hand away.

"Tell him to make a right on this road," her mother says. "Pass two traffic lights, take a left and then head in toward the plaza. He will see the crowd by then."

"Will there be a stage of some sort?" Dolores asks. If she sticks to formalities, she won't have to confront this fear. This is just another performance. Just another job.

Dolores' mother shakes her head in disappointment. She dabs the handkerchief against her forehead.

"We should talk about Melody—"

"There is nothing to say," Dolores cuts her off. She feels so exposed. Without a skin, she can't conceal her emotions. Instead she must rely on this coldness. "Just let me know if there are any unusual requests."

Dolores' mother turns to her. There is no anger in her expression, only the perpetual sadness Dolores grew up seeing most her life. Her mother reaches and takes the mask from Dolores' hand. She uses the edge of her handkerchief to remove a smudge on the mask and gently places it back on her daughter's lap.

"Tell the driver it's just up ahead," her mother says.

To be a teenager and forced to work funerals was something Dolores had hated more than anything. She resented her mother for it. The university became Dolores' only refuge, a place where she thought she could reinvent herself. Then she met Melody and was led right back to Dolientes and the ritual of the weeper. With Melody by her side, Dolores believed in the role of a sort of healer until the university became too small for her. Dolores wanted more and Melody didn't understand.

A crowd forms in front of the plaza. Large families with kids running around. Young and old. There are no canopies to hide from the blistering sun. A couple of young boys hand out paper fans with the words *La Cruz 13* printed on them. She recognizes some of their faces. Neighbors. Former students now adults with their own kids. Where does Melody hide among these people? Dolores seeks her out like a fool. Desperate for a sign that she is doing the right thing.

She takes a large sip of water. Her hands start to shake. Melody will appear. It's only a matter of time. And what will Dolores do? This dance will not absolve the countless ways she has betrayed her community. Nor will the act stop her from continuing. That is the bitter truth. When Dolores reaches to open the car door, her mother grabs her arm.

"Melody never stopped asking for you. She always followed your career," her mother says. "I know she loved you."

Dolores inhales deeply. She will not cry, although her mother's words feel like blows to her stomach.

"I'm here, am I not?" She appeals to her mother to let her get out of the car. "I loved her, too."

"Yes, you are here," her mother says. "For Melody, then."

Dolores takes the Pascola mask and places it behind her head, then steps out of the car.

A woman greets her and leads her to the center of the plaza. She is talking while Dolores walks as if entering a fog. Faces stare at her, waiting for her to begin. None of the faces is the person she desperately needs to see. Her mother has joined the crowd. The handkerchief already captures her tears.

The service begins. A young woman with long braids steps in front, holding a piece of paper.

"We come together to mourn and to remember The Disappeared. They were thirteen. Eleven students. Two professors," she reads from the paper. "These thirteen worked together to stop the violence being inflicted in our home. They loved La Cruz and defended it to the very end. The cowards who murdered our loved ones will fail because hate always fails."

Another student, this time a boy, steps forward. He doesn't shy away from his emotions. Tears slide down his face. "Remember their names: Joaquín Villareal, Carlos Guzmán, Jesús García, Giovanni Bautista, Antonio Nava, Rocío Rivera, Oscar Ruiz, Angela Navarette, Brenda Ramírez, Vicky Elizalde, Israel Logardo. And our beloved instructors, Pablo Fernández and Melody Flores."

Dolores searches for Melody, for the face of the woman she loved. To see her long, flowing, wavy hair one more time. Melody does not appear. Only the people of La Cruz stare back at her with anticipation. There are no flowers. No glitzy stage. No drinks. Just a crowd with no answers, seeking justice. The prodigal daughter returns. What does Dolores have to offer? Will her dance be enough? Nothing will ever bring the thirteen back. Nothing will bring Melody back to her. There is only the ritual.

A man begins to play the violin at a quick pace, soon followed by another man. A student joins in with a small harp and another with a hide drum. They nod at Dolores and she begins. She stomps her feet along with the rhythmic drum. Her moves are awkward at first, not smooth like when she is The Selena™. Dolores tries to find the right rhythm, to follow the music of the violins and harp. Soon she is in step. She shakes the bells attached to her pants. Her feet are bare and the dirt floor is hot. She continues. She sings ancient songs, not loud and vibrant, low so that only the violin players can hear. A ringing of bells echoes as she shakes the cocoons filled with stones.

The dance goes on and Dolores doesn't stop even when her mother asks her to rest. She stomps and turns, dancing toward the musicians and twirling away. For Dolores, the crowd no longer exists. It is just her and the movements that matter now. The more she dances, the harder she prays that her steps will bring Melody. She needs to see her one last time. Why not here, in her home? Why not in front of these people? The dance becomes a conjuring spell she's created to will Melody back to her.

Come to me, Melody, she prays. *This is for you. Come back to me one last time. Send me a sign that all is forgiven.*

Dolores closes her eyes and prays some more. She opens her eyes and searches for Melody in the crowd. She sees nothing. It is hypnotic, this dance, with its stomping feet and ringing bells. If she stomps harder, perhaps Melody will come to her. If she concentrates, falls deeper into the notes being played on the instruments. Perhaps. Dolores is no longer a Doliente. She is the Pascola, the mountain spirit. She continues until the sun sets. Still, there is no Melody. She stomps harder. The bells ring louder. There is only this dance. She spins and twirls. Faster. Dizzying. The musicians try to follow her lead. The bells ring throughout La Cruz.

When she finally stops, no one claps. The only sound is her heavy breathing. Dolores looks down at her feet. They are covered in dust. The skin is breaking. Her heart is sore. She failed. Melody is no more. There is only the dirt and the bells on her pants. There is only the inky-blue sky and this consuming guilt.

When her mother approaches, Dolores is unable to hold back the tears. Her mother hugs her and Dolores falls into the embrace. She feels small, weak. When was the last time Dolores felt this warmth? The last time she allowed this touch? They walk like this to her car.

"Dolores, come back home," her mother says. "We need you here. *I* need you."

She is unable to face her mother. Her request feels insurmountable. What will Dolores be returning to but despair? A Doliente is meant to comfort. Who will alleviate this heavy heart of hers? It's too late. She made the decision to leave and there is no sign indicating she should stay. This guilt she feels will be her armor, her new skin.

She looks around. Young mothers hold their babies tight. Students cry. Neighbors she hasn't seen in ages comfort each other. Some are angry, and that anger will propel them to act. Dolores can join them. Take up where Melody left off. Can't she? She can leave the world she built for herself behind. Her apartment made of silver. Her skins. Dolores can return to find her home again, to be a true Doliente. It's not possible, not when she lacks the courage to take such a step.

"I can't," Dolores says.

Her mother grips her tightly.

"I'm so sorry." Dolores pushes her away and rushes into the car before breaking down.

"Where to, Miss?" the driver asks.

"Take me home," Dolores answers. Her mother stands by the car, her arms crossed in front of her.

As the car pulls away, an alert comes in from the Codigo5G. "*New Request.*"

Melody once said to her that she was stronger than both of them. That she can carry the weight. She was wrong. She is weak. Dolores will continue to be a cog in this corrupt machine. She will continue to live in her skins.

Dolores turns in her seat and faces the town. The car slowly bumps forward on the dirt road until the buildings fade away and there is nothing left to see.

Excerpt from *Before We Became a New People*

Ivelisse Rodriguez

Ponce, Puerto Rico
July 25, 1898

It took twenty-eight men. Only twenty-eight to capture an island, to plant a flag, to alter the course of history. The Americans first landed in Guánica, two days before they easily strolled into the city of Ponce. And the inhabitants, doomed to repeat history, did not assemble when they heard the shots, surely coming from Ponce Harbor. And Ponce, *La Perla del Sur, La Ciudad Señorial*, the second city of Puerto Rico, shimmering like a pearl on the Caribbean Sea, was not defended by anyone; no one ripped off nightshirts and knocked on neighbors' doors to rouse anyone; no one rode horses at breakneck speed to the harbor to defend Ponce and shoot at least one American.

The only one who came to defend was the spirit of Agüeybaná, who first encountered Ponce de León on these Borinken shores in 1508. Agüeybaná showed a friendly hand, when Agüeybaná should have pulled Ponce de León in with that outstretched hand, smile still on his face, and swiftly and repeatedly stabbed Ponce de León in the throat. Since 1510, since that inglorious death at the hands of the Spanish, directly or indirectly, Agüeybaná has guarded the beaches with his poisoned arrow tips at the ready. For those who storm the island, the poison is directed at their spirits, their limbs, their hearts.

The first on the ground, who surely missed Agüeybaná's spirit, was Tom Waite, who had only seen cranberry farms in Warrens, Wisconsin, before he journeyed on the sea. Because Tom Waite traded the grass for the sea when he was rejected by the US Army, he needed to be first, impatient to feel the land under him. On the sea, for the first time, Tom Waite was accosted by his minuteness, which disturbed him the entire journey. So, the closer they got to the shore, the more substantial he felt. On that farmland in Warrens, Wisconsin, all he had ever felt was his vastness, attuned with that firmament.

When they landed, he wavered for a moment, unsure of where he was. Because he had been watching the flamboyan tree in the distance, the closer they got, the more the tree's densely populated red leaves reminded him of the cranberry fields. He only needed to close his eyes for a second before opening them again to no longer see Ponce ahead of him. Instead, he saw Warrens all around him, the leaves of the flamboyan tree bending to the earth, forming a canopy of cranberries.

His heavy leather boots met the sand first, which still rolled like the sea. And he sloshed through the sand like he did the cranberry bogs. He mumbled, "Mama," to himself, expecting his robust, white-haired mother to call him in for supper, like when he was a boy and he used to run to the furthest regions of the farm to see how far he could go and still hear his mother's voice. His mother's voice was like the laundry flapping in the wind. Up, up and away.

As he lurched forward, toward the grass, he knew he should have already slung his gun into his arms and pointed it at the distance for anyone who passed within their line of sight. But he needed to reach the grass, and when he did, it was not enough for his feet to touch the earth, next were his knees, then his elbows and his forehead.

Right before Tom Waite's fellow soldiers closed ranks in front of him, to not only protect him, but to also reinforce their impenetrability, Agüeybaná pointed his arrows and shot through the feet of Tom Waite, which would one day make them ripple with pain, then a numbness and then an amputation. And upon awareness of each, Tom Waite would remember this day and the gratitude of feeling what was under his feet.

Reginald Davis had not volunteered to get on the small boat to shore, but he was sent out first. Immediately, he was distracted by the pull of the air, the familiar sweat of his boyhood Florida summers, his begrudgings melting in the face of the sweltering Puerto Rican sun. Back home, on days like this, he had waited for the cooling rains that passed every afternoon, and he wondered if it was like that here too—that god, the universe or whatever made the world burn would release the valve, offering rain as a respite.

When Agüeybaná spied Reginald Davis, he mistook him for a Congo, a Lucimí or a Yoruban, who also came across the sea, but who were also led by chains like the Taínos after Agüeybaná opened the door. But here Reginald Davis stood, a sign of survival. Though he was not of these shores, Agüeybaná greeted him like an old friend. When Reginald started to transform in front of him, his skinny chest filling out, his rifle turning into a machete, the gloom of exile falling all over him,

Agüeybaná put down his poisoned arrows and found himself chanting praises to Ogún, the Yoruban god of war and iron. Agüeybaná was no longer alone. He had just been a man, and now here was a god. Ogún was one of the first orishas on earth. When the orishas descended, they could not move forward on earth because of the dense shrubbery. They all had to wait for Ogún to clear the path with his machete. Along with his machete, Ogún brings justice. In courts, people swear on his name to speak the truth, not risking Ogún's wrath by daring to lie.

Agüeybaná was heartened. When he let the Spaniards in, he thought it was the best way to make peace. But peace only led to murder. With Ogún by his side, they would finally win with the violence that always won.

Lázaro Santiago, who should have been a Mexican-Mexican, not a Mexican-Texan, had joined the Navy to get away from the land that was no longer his. On his first tour, pushing off from the Gulf Coast, Lázaro waved to former Mexico. And he ran away to the heart of darkness because his daddy and his brother almost got lynched outside of a cantina that they had spent most of their lives outside of. The US Navy took Lázaro but not knowing what to do with him, they placed him with a black regiment. The US Navy took Lázaro because he could speak Spanish. It was Lázaro who would have to shout out commands to any Spaniards or *criollos* that came to fight. But to everyone's surprise, no one was waiting at the beach ready to fight. As he helped shield Tom Waite, as he waited for anyone, anyone at all to show up, he looked up and down the beach and started to relax and swung his gun over his shoulder.

He went to wipe his sweat, as it was as hot as former Mexico, and when his hand was on the nether portions of his face, almost ready to wipe that sweat on his pants, the heat fluttered in sheets; Agüeybaná's image slowly emerged as if he were made of water.

As if Puerto Rico were still Borinken, Agüeybaná was naked, except for the *guanín* around his neck which signified his title of *cacique*.

Lázaro immediately recognized Agüeybaná as the history that he was—the history of men, women and children easily wiped from history. And that piercing thought that came up now and again bubbled up, that maybe he should not have joined the US Navy. That he was helping to bring the only thing they could bring to the world.

So he found himself walking backwards. But Agüeybaná stopped him.

And Lázaro watched Agüeybaná go down on his knees as out of Lázaro came the last *tlatoani* Cuauhtémoc, who defended Tenochtitlán against the Spaniards. Even before Cuauhtémoc became emperor, he knew the Spaniards were not gods or allies like so many thought, but merely men and enemies. And Cuauhtémoc, for sure, knew it again when his feet were burned when the found treasure within Tenochtitlán did not line up with the riches the Spanish had imagined.

Cuauhtémoc saluted Agüeybaná, and for the first time in all these centuries, Agüeybaná felt a reprieve. Cuauhtémoc was the Descending Eagle. Agüeybaná was honored that such a brave leader like Cuauhtémoc would even salute him, recognize him. Cuauhtémoc was immortalized as a "winner in defeat." Agüeybaná was sure he was the progenitor of this Puerto Rican né Borinken docility. He did this, he stood helpless before what the sea brought, and they all died. He was not a Great Sun protecting the nation, but he was the tomfool who opened the doors and let them saunter in. But here was Cuauhtémoc, outstretching his arms to Agüeybaná, thankful for his act of bravery against Tom Waite.

But the coming of Ogún and Cuauhtémoc was a harbinger that Agüeybaná alone was not enough. And just like Cuauhtémoc knew who the Spaniards were, Cuauhtémoc knew who the Americans were.

And now that Cuauhtémoc and Ogún joined Agüeybaná, it was okay that they were the only ones to fight for Ponce at the arrival of the Americans. As if the Americans could feel them, they, one-by-one, started shooting at what they were sure was nothing at all.

Contributor Bios

JOSÉ ALANIZ

Born and raised in Edinburg, TX, Alaniz has worn a few hats over the years: journalist, cartoonist and spinner of yarns. His work has appeared in, among others, *The Berkeley Review, The Mesquite Review, Tales From La Vida: A Latinx Comics Anthology* (2018) and *BorderX: A Crisis in Graphic Detail* (2020). He is also a professor in the Department of Slavic Languages and Literatures and the Department of Cinema & Media Studies (adjunct) at the University of Washington, Seattle. In 2020 he published his first comics collection, *The Phantom Zone and Other Stories* (Amatl Comix) and in 2023 his second, *The Compleat Moscow Calling* (Amatl Comix). His first prose collection, *Puro Pinche True Fictions,* is forthcoming from Flowersong Press.

CLOUD DELFINA CARDONA

Cardona (she/they) is a poet born and raised in San Antonio, Texas. She received her B.A. from St. Mary's University in English Communication Arts and her MFA in Creative Writing from Texas State University. She is the author of *What Remains*, winner of the 2020 Host Publications Chapbook Award. Her poems have appeared in *Apogee Journal*, *Cosmo-*

nauts Avenue, *Salt Hill Journal* and many more. Cardona co-founded *Chifladazine*, a zine that highlights creative work by Latinas and Latinxs, in 2013 alongside Laura Valdez. In Fall 2019, she co-founded *Infrarrealista Review*, a literary journal for Texan writers, with Juania Rivas Vázquez.

V. CASTRO

Castro was born in San Antonio, Texas, to Mexican-American parents. She's been writing horror stories since she was a child, always fascinated by Mexican folklore and the urban legends of Texas. Castro now lives in the United Kingdom with her family, writing and traveling with her children.

ADRIAN ERNESTO CEPEDA

Cepeda is the author of *Flashes & Verses . . . Becoming Attractions* from Unsolicited Press, *Between the Spine* from Picture Show Press, *Speaking con su Sombra* with Alegría Publishing, *La Belle Ajar & We Are the Ones Possessed* from CLASH Books and his 6th poetry collection *La Lengua Inside Me* will be published by FlowerSong Press in 2023. Adrian lives with his wife in Los Angeles and with their adorably spoiled cat Woody Gold.

ANN DÁVILA CARDINAL

Dávila Cardinal is a novelist and Director of Recruitment for Vermont College of Fine Arts (VCFA) where she also earned her MFA in Writing. Ann's first novel, *Sister Chicas* was co-written with Jane Alberdeston Coralin and Lisa Alvarado, and was released by New American Library in 2006. Her next novel, a horror YA work titled *Five Midnights* was released by Tor Teen on June 4, 2019. *Five Midnights* won the 2020 International Latino Book Award in the category of Best Young Adult Fantasy & Adventure, an AudioFile's Earphones Award for the audiobook and was finalist for the Bram Stoker Award. The story continues in *Category Five*, also from Tor Teen, released on June 2, 2020. Category Five is a 2021 nominee for the same International Latino Book Award category. Her next young adult horror novel, *Breakup From Hell*, will be released by HarperCollins on January 3, 2023. Her first adult novel, the Puerto Rican magical realist mystery *The Storyteller's Death*, was released by Sourcebooks Landmark on October 4, 2022.

RUBÉN DEGOLLADO

Degollado's work has appeared in *Bilingual Review/Revista Bilingüe, Beloit Fiction Journal*, *Gulf Coast, Hayden's Ferry Review, Image, Relief* and the anthologies *Living Beyond Borders* and *Nepantla Familias.* His YA novel, *Throw,* was published in 2019 and won the Texas Institute of Letters 2020 Award for Best Young Adult Book, was included on the Texas Library Association 2020 TAYSHAS list of best books for teen readers and was a *Christianity Today* 2020 Book of Merit. Rubén's debut literary novel, *The Family Izquierdo,* published in 2022 by W.W. Norton, was a *New York Times* Book Review Editor's Choice, was included on *Kirkus Review's* Best Fiction of 2022 and appears on the Pen-Faulkner Award Longlist.

ESTELLA GONZALEZ

Gonzalez is the author of the award-winning short story collection, *Chola Salvation*, published by Arte Público Press in April 2021. Her work has also been published by *Kweli Journal*, *Huizache*, *Asteri(x) Journal* and other literary journals. Her poetry has been anthologized in *What They Leave Behind: A Latinx Anthology* and *Nasty Women Poets: An Unapologetic Anthology of Subversive Verse* by Lost Horse Press. Her stories have garnered numerous distinctions and awards including Cornell University's Philip Freund Prize in Creative Writing, a Pushcart Prize "Special Mention" and a "Reading Notable" for *The Best American Non-Required Reading*. At the 24th annual International Latino Book Awards, she received a Rising Star award for *Chola Salvation*, which won gold medals for Best First Book and Best Short Story Collection. Estella was born and raised in East Los Angeles which inspires her writing. She received her B.A. in English from Northwestern University and her MFA in fiction from Cornell University. She lives in Tucson with her husband and two cats.

PEDRO INIGUEZ

Iniguez (he/him) is a speculative fiction writer and painter from Los Angeles. His work has appeared in *Nightmare Magazine*, *Tales from OmniPark*, *Tiny Nightmares*, *Star*Line*, *Space and Time Magazine*, *Helios Quarterly* and *Speculative Fiction for Dreamers*. He can be found online at Pedroiniguezauthor.com.

MARCOS DAMIÁN LEÓN

León is a teacher and writer from the Salinas Valley. He holds an MFA from The University of California, Riverside, and is pursuing a Ph.D. at Texas Tech University. He is working on a young adult novel about a pair of *primos* who must decide what kind of men they want to become. He can be found @damleon on Instagram and @damleon24 on Twitter.

SYDNEY MACIAS

Macias is a practicing novel writer whose interests take form in metaphysical settings. Her work explores large casts of ambiguous characters dealing with themes of grief, identity and power. She received a Bachelor of Fine Arts with an emphasis in Writing from the School of the Art Institute of Chicago.

Her experience includes being a Senior Editor and contributor to *Mouth Magazine,* judging the *Writer's Games* for Writer's Workout and being an Assistant Editor for the speculative fiction publisher Mythic Delirium. Follow her on Instagram at @_syd.mac_.

OSCAR MANCINAS

Mancinas is Rarámuri-Chicanx poet, author, teacher and scholar. His poetic works include the chapbooks *Jaula* (Gasher Press, 2020) and *Roto: A Mex-Tape* (rinky dink press, 2020), as well as the full-length collection *des____: papeles, palabras, & poems from the desert* (Tolsun Books, 2022). His debut collection of short fiction, *To Live and Die in El Valle* (Arte Público Press, 2020) won a 2021 Border Regional Library Association Southwest Book Award. He's a proud resident of Mesa, Arizona's Washington-Escobedo Neighborhood.

RICHIE NARVAEZ

Narvaez was born and raised in Williamsburg, Brooklyn. Narvaez received a master's degree from the State University of New York at Stony Brook and attended the Humber School for Writers on a scholarship. His first book, *Roachkiller and Other Stories,* received the Spinetingler Award for Best Collection. His book *Noiryoirican* was nominated for an Anthony Award, and his book *Holly Hernandez and the Death of Disco* received an Agatha Award and an Anthony Award.

MÓNICA TERESA ORTIZ

ortiz is a poet and interdisciplinary artist born and raised in the rural panhandle of Texas. Currently, ortiz is a journalist in residence with the Freedomways Reporting Project, an artist in residence with UT Austin's Planet Texas 2050 initiative and has work forthcoming in Hayden Ferry's Review and Scalawag. The author of the poetry collections Muted Blood and Autobiography of a Semiromantic Anarchist, follow them on Twitter @elgallosalvaje or on substack at elgallosalvaje.substack.com.

TONI MARGARITA PLUMMER

Plummer was born and raised in the San Gabriel Valley of Los Angeles, the daughter of a Mexican immigrant mother and white father. She is the author of the story collection *The Bolero of Andi Rowe,* a Macondo Fellow, and a graduate of the Master of Professional Writing Program at USC. Her first horror story won *Somos En Escrito*'s 2021 Extra Fiction Contest, and her short fiction has also appeared in *Aster(ix), The Latino Book Review* and *LatineLit.* After moving to New York City, Plummer embarked on a career in publishing and now serves on the board of Latinx in Publishing. She lives in the Hudson Valley.

RUBEN QUESADA

Quesada is editor of *Latinx Poetics: The Art of Poetry,* author of *Revelations, Next Extinct Mammal,* and translator of *Selected Translations of Luis Cernuda.* His writing appears in *Harvard Review Best American Poetry, New York Times Magazine* and *American Poetry Review.* He was an editor for *The Rumpus, The Kenyon Review, AGNI* and *Pleiades.* He lives in Chicago.

MONIQUE QUINTANA

Quintana is a Xicana from Fresno, CA, and is the author of Cenote City (Clash Books). Her work has been supported by Yaddo, The Sundress Academy for the Arts, The Community of Writers and The Kimmel Harding Nelson Center. She was the inaugural winner of Amplify's Writer of Color Fellowship and is a contributing editor at *Luna Luna* Magazine, where she writes book reviews, artist interviews and personal essays. You can find her at moniquequintana.com.

LILLIAM RIVERA

Rivera is an award-winning author of the young adult novels *We Light Up the Sky*, *Never Look Back*, *Dealing in Dreams*, *The Education of Margot Sanchez* and the middle grade Goldie Vance series. Her latest middle grade novel *Barely Floating* will be out Fall 2023 by Kokila Books. Her novel *Never Look Back*, a Pura Belpré Honor book, is slated for an Amazon movie adaptation. Rivera lives in Los Angeles.

IVELISSE RODRIGUEZ

Rodriguez's debut short story collection *Love War Stories* was a 2019 PEN/Faulkner finalist and a 2018 *Foreword Reviews* INDIES finalist. It was noted as a must read or best book of the year in over thirty publications, including *O* magazine, *Women's Health*, *Good Housekeeping*, *Cosmopolitan* and more. She is a contributing arts editor for the *Boston Review*, where she acquires fiction. She is a 2022 Letras Boricuas fellow and a Tanne Foundation award winner, a Kimbilio fellow and a VONA/Voices alum. She earned an M.F.A. in creative writing from Emerson College and a Ph.D. in English-creative writing from the University of Illinois at Chicago.

FLOR SALCEDO

Salcedo was born and raised in the border town of El Paso, TX, the setting for "La Llorona Happenings." She is a computer programmer living in Austin, Texas dreaming of the day she can transition to writing full time. Her work has appeared in *The Ocotillo Review,* the anthology *Foreshadow: Stories to Celebrate the Magic of Reading and Writing YA*, and the Latine anthology *Where Monsters Lurk & Magic Hides.*

LETICIA URIETA

Urieta (she/her/hers) is a Tejana writer from Austin, TX. She works as a teaching artist in the Austin community and is the Program Director for Austin Bat Cave. Her chapbook, *The Monster*, is out now from LibroMobile Press. Her hybrid collection, *Las Criaturas*, which was a finalist for the Sergio Troncoso Award for Best First Book of Fiction 2022 from the Texas Institute of Letters, is out now from FlowerSong Press.

Contributor Notes

JOSÉ ALANIZ

"Tamales" brings together my family history with sci-fi tropes. The italicized sections are taken from life. Mars and the cohete are my family's immigration story filtered through Bradbury. Fortunately, my family—among them my mother—made it across safely. Here we are, and here I am.

CLOUD DELFINA CARDONA

"What I Know" is a poem inspired by my uncle and grandmother. They passed away when I was very little so I never knew them personally. I tend to think about what these people were like while alive. It's hard to know how you would get along with ancestors when all you know is formed from the perspectives of the living. There's so much I wish I could ask them. This poem was pieced together with the little bits I know about them. In the poem "Eternal Life" I recall how I distinctly remember learning about eternity in elementary school and spiraling about it at night. I couldn't wrap my head around it and yet other people around me seemed to accept it without question. I thought about death a lot as a kid and suffered from intrusive thoughts. Thinking about my loved ones dying was like a private ritual I hated. It gave me so much anxiety. This poem is inspired by my experiences in Catholic school and existential anxiety.

V. CASTRO

"The Boy Called Chupa" was born from frustration. It is easy to watch atrocities unfold, but often we look away and think nothing more of it. As a mother of three it angered me to read about so many children in dire need alone at the border. There were also many families being torn apart. People fleeing for their lives and seeking to create a decent livelihood should not be a crime. Children are innocent and should be treated as such. As a Latina writer I often create stories about being the other. This is no exception. You get a glimpse who really is the monster. Often, it depends on the storyteller. Because I have the privilege of writing these tales, I chose to explore a different perspective; one that is not based on white supremacy.

ADRIAN ERNESTO CEPEDA

"A Night of Screams" was inspired by a true story that happened during the Naughts. We went to a house in Austin, TX and were asked to go into the house next door, but we never did. It always haunted me. I wish I had gone in. What would I have found? This night stayed with me. I wrote this story to bring out the terror I often imagined.

ANN DÁVILA CARDINAL

I wrote "What the Hurricane Took" as a direct response to the forty-eight hours after Hurricane María when I didn't know if my family was alive or dead. Anyone who loved someone on the island that September understands the feeling of complete terror and helplessness. It was nothing compared to those who lived through it, but horrifying nonetheless. My cousin Tere Dávila is a writer in Puerto Rico, and since she was my main contact during it all (and since she and I both write darkass things), I wanted to honor her with this story.

RUBÉN DEGOLLADO

"Migrants" is a departure for me as an author. Though I've always loved a good zombie story, I've never written one. It's also different because everything I write is in the same fictional universe and revolves around the Izquierdo family. There are supernatural elements in my stories, but they occur in the world we know, not in a world overrun with zombies. Aside from one season in *Fear the Walking Dead*, I've never seen any zombie stories set along the border, and there are so many stories to be told here. Along similar lines, I also enjoy watching *Narcos* and have seen every show and every season. Then it hit me: add elements of both genres into "Migrants" and see what happens. Certainly there is commentary about border policies in the story, but more importantly, I wanted to tell a story about one individual trying to survive, while also helping others, despite utter hopelessness.

ESTELLA GONZALEZ

Is horror ever ordinary? Or banal? The everyday horror of patriarchy and forced gender roles can be as traumatic as the supernatural kind. Ordinary events, like a Mexican mother-in-law's visit, initiated "Chola Salvation."

The summer she came to town, my first marriage was coming to an end. We had kept her in the dark about our marital struggles. One night, when she saw my husband—her son—ironing his own shirt, she turned to me. "I always iron my husband's shirts," she said. Her remark added to the horror and guilt I felt as a Mexican wife and daughter about to divorce (I still am the only divorcee in my Catholic family). Deeply inculcated marianismo, an ideology that embraces female passivity, hyperfemininity and silence, effectively muted me. Contemporaneously, Frida Kahlo's artwork was feeding the Chicana arts zeitgeist. Her artistic output in the midst of her own miserable marriage inspired me to channel my frustration with the impossible expectations of a "proper Mexican" daughter and wife. I resurrected Frida from the dead and paired her with the feminist version of the Virgen de Guadalupe. As a supernatural duo, they would guide and save my protagonist, and possibly others, from a quinceañera and other rituals that reinforced an unnatural, sometimes horrifying, version of womanhood.

PEDRO INIGUEZ

"Purveyors and Puppets" was inspired by the political news pundits and ideologues on nightly television that spew their manufactured vitriol, sowing the seeds of hate, xenophobia and distrust for their public to consume. Sometimes their hate spills out through real-life acts of violence, committed by people so invested in their lies and rhetoric, that they see other humans as mortal enemies. I took that concept and created this story, putting it through a sort of nihilistic, cosmic horror lens.

MARCOS DAMIÁN LEÓN

"Indian Blood" started with an idea: field workers being bled to produce vegetables and wealth. I grew up hearing from older family members that picking vegetables in the fields was slowly killing them. It became clear that they and other field workers were giving their bodies—their blood, so to speak—to grow and pick and package food necessary for our society to function, but they often couldn't even afford to buy the food they helped produce. I thought this was a Chicano issue and that our entire community would care about and defend my hardworking elders, but I grew older and realized that my community was at an intersection of race and class that made their struggles unimportant to Chicanos with power. Farmworkers are often seen by other Mexicans and Chicanos as "indios", and the Chicanos elected to public office are more concerned with their own class aspirations and performing false community solidarity than with defending poor indios. Classic horror, like Soylent Green, plays with the idea of making people into food, but this isn't some hypothetical dystopia—people are being abused and thrown away by the agriculture industry that feeds us, and it seems like no one cares to defend those field workers. To me, real-world horror lies in betrayal from the people we trusted to support us.

SYDNEY MACIAS

"It Said 'Bellevue'" was originally inspired by a reading in a psychology class. It discussed the ways in which the historic Bellevue hospital in New York has been a groundbreaking nexus for medical achievement. The language was absolutely reverent and it discussed how people from all over the world came to be treated at this hospital. It got me thinking: what if the hospital treated not only people from any country, but spirits and creatures of the otherworldly? I waited months before actually putting words down on the page because I felt I didn't have all the pieces. That was until I started taking a class on Latinx history when I found myself connecting to my narrator as I used this story of natural and supernatural borders to relate to my own identity and cultural borders.

OSCAR MANCINAS

Whether due to colonialism, capitalism or the environmental fallout from each, migration and displacement form inescapable parts of my peoples' histories. We confront these monsters, first, in our ancestral homes, and then again, and again and again, wherever we go, each time losing something we cannot recover; our diaspora a kind of unending haunting. Growing up, I'd overhear stories about people in my family who had to move to stay alive, and, usually, these stories were from the perspectives of the wanderers: where they went, what they did, what they missed. "Cruz & Me," however, is meant to represent the other side—el otro lado—of these stories. What do people do, what can they do, when they must wait? Taking the shape of a flash fiction nightmare, "Cruz & Me" seizes on the void left behind by those who cross over to the unknown.

RICHIE NARVAEZ

"A Thing with Feathers" was inspired by my struggles as a writer, struggles I hear echoed again and again when I talk to writer friends and on social media. Much of the dream of success for a writer (or artist of any kind) is based on a deep association with and a devotion to hope,. I've often wondered if that devotion to something that is so often destroyed and then so often renewed is not a little corrosive, even addictive. So, this made me think of how this artistic addiction might make the artist vulnerable, enough to become prey to sinister forces that exist off this pulsing sense of hope . . . sinister forces such as agents, editors, publishers.

In visualizing the horror for my story, I thought of course of Emily Dickenson's poem "'Hope' is the thing with feathers." Even in her poem, she places "hope" in quotation marks, as if it were something suspect, and she describes it as a birdlike thing that "perches in the soul," sits there inside you and "never stops - at all." Many see the poem as inspirational, hope as indomitable. But it's not too much of a stretch to see it also as something sinister, an ever-present thing that never wants to let you stop feeling it!

MÓNICA TERESA ORTIZ

One of my favorite works is Tomás Rivera's *. . .And the Earth Did Not Devour Him*. Rivera was from Crystal City, and wrote these heartbreaking beautiful vignettes centered around labor, migration, family, set in South Texas in the 40s and 50s. I love that these stories are fractured and involve the act of remembering, as well as naming the conditions of migrant farmworkers during a specific time frame. The 90s in rural Texas, in the Panhandle, witnessed many changes on a local scale to a global scale. So, setting "A Curious Encounter" during that time of transition felt important to me, and writing about the place and the landscape where I grew up, with characters whose experiences as farmers, Catholics, migrants influenced a perception of place, and their relationship to each other and to the land. The idea came from a story my dad told me about my grandfather, who was a cowboy in South Texas, and while checking traps one day, he and his friend spotted a creature that they had never seen before. I wanted to play with the horror genre because I am a fan of it. I want there to be more stories about the Texas Panhandle that don't involve the colonial framework of frontiers or pioneers and that don't feed into Dobie Paisano's Texas folklore.

TONI MARGARITA PLUMMER

In "Night Shifts" I knew the setting first—a hostess club in downtown LA based on a place where I worked for one night! I decided the main character should be a vampire who is a dance hostess, and I loved imagining how this very old being would relate to the characters around her.

RUBEN QUESADA

My poem "1985" imagines the announcement of Rock Hudson's death. Hudson was a small-town boy who became a movie star. He was born on November 17, 1925, in Winnetka, Illinois—only fifteen miles north of where I live in Chicago.

From 1984 to 1985, he was an actor on Dynasty, a television series. In May 1984, he attended President Ronald Reagan's White House state dinner. Three weeks later, Hudson was diagnosed with HIV. Reagan would not address the AIDS epidemic for another two years. In October 1985, he died of an AIDS-related illness. He requested to be cremated. There was no funeral.

MONIQUE QUINTANA

In recent years, I have been interested in interrogating and archiving public spaces in my hometown of Fresno, located in California's Central Valley. While the Rainbow Ballroom has historically been a popular dance venue for young brown people, it is also essential to my personal history, where my mother and father first met. I use the folk image of an animalistic figure preying on young women, a narrative prevalent in Texas, where my grandmothers are from, to explore a teenage girl's fascination with storytelling and the darker aspects of desire in "A Curious Encounter."

LILLIAM RIVERA

I started working on a version of "Between Going and Staying" back in 2015 when I attended the Clarion science fiction and fantasy workshop in San Diego. The story was really my way of working through the horrific tragedy that occurred to the 43 Ayotzinapa students who disappeared in Mexico in 2014. Set in a futuristic world, the story centers around Dolores, a doliente who makes money as a hired mourner to drug dealers. Guilt presents itself when Dolores must travel back to her home to mourn the death of her ex-lover. The story plays around with the idea of tragedy as a commodity. When stripped of its evils, can a person return to their true calling? Can they let go of the lure of capitalism to see what their gift is truly meant for? To me, the horror is found in Dolores and the masks she keeps wearing.

IVELISSE RODRIGUEZ

Before We Became a New People focuses on the 1898 invasion of Puerto Rico by the United States. What I wanted to capture is how Puerto Ricans did not fight against the US invasion (because they thought it was liberation from Spain) and how this connects to how Agüeybaná received Ponce de León. There are two instances of invasion, and none is handled with defense. This then connects to this idea of Puerto Rican docility that intellectuals like Antonio S. Pedreira and René Marqués examine. So, I started to think about what would Agüeybaná do now, on July 25, 1898, if he could have a re-do? He would hope to do something differently and to recognize the danger that is coming. He needs a posse, though, to help shift the way that this invasion unfolds. So Ogún and Cuauhtémoc come to help Agüeybaná to warn the people about what is to come in the hopes of rallying them.

FLOR SALCEDO

"La Llorona Happenings" is a fictional story based on Mexican folklore and inspired by real-life events. Aiming to capture both the magic and whirlwind of growing up in the Mexican-American barrio of a border town in which folklore and real-life mix, it captures a moment of lost innocence in which a child shaped by the fear of lore monsters, realizes that people are monsters, too.

LETICIA URIETA

"Detached" is a piece centered on the very real horrors of inhabiting a body in pain. I wanted to explore how chronic and acute pain can make a person detach from their body, but also what power is there in a body in pain. What can be unlocked in the body when pain strips away the pretense of politeness and following the rules? As someone who experiences this type of pain, I was motivated to explore these ideas, especially as they affect my body as a woman and how I am supposed to suppress and endure pain quietly.